Dear Gurlie

(gurlé: pronounced girl)

Robin Roberts

Dear Gurlé

~~DEAR BLACK FEMALE~~
~~DEAR WHITE FEMALE~~
~~DEAR LATINA FEMALE~~
~~DEAR INDIAN FEMALE~~
~~DEAR ASIAN FEMALE~~
~~DEAR MULTICULTURAL FEMALE~~

There is a HURT ~~girl~~ gurlé inside
ALL of us.

Written by Caprice Lamor

Dear Gurlé

For more information visit:

www.byclamor.com

Printed in the United States of America

First Trade Edition: October, 2020

ISBN: 978-1-7355448-1-6

Book Production: Marvin D. Cloud

Editor: Calabria D. Turner

Cover Art: Salaam Muhammad

Cover Design: Ugens Toussaint

Cover Models: Yolanda Burgett and Paris Johnson

Thirty-One Letters
Proverbs 31

There is a Virtuous Woman Inside of YOU!

About Thirty-One Letters

I wanted to reach young and mature women of all backgrounds, ages and ethnicities who live in a world filled with hate, sexism and division, due to their colors of skin, love preferences, gender, religions, beliefs or practices. I recognized that no matter what is culturally different about each of us, there is one thing we all can relate to and that we each share in common, which is being a FEMALE. Most females have been or are currently scarred, hurt, damaged and misjudged. They have been depressed, suicidal, misunderstood and broken, mistreated, unpopular, confused and abandoned, abused and unwanted. Many women have felt unloved, suffered from low self-esteem, identity issues and loneliness. I went through the majority of these things listed, and I knew that if I've experienced this, then there are more young ladies and women who are also experiencing the very things I've gotten through and continually am healing from today. There is no greater role on this earth than being a FEMALE who develops into a Daughter, Sister, Aunt, Wife, Mother, Grandmother and Friend. We were created by God because he knew that our presence on this earth was needed. We serve a PURPOSE in this world! We are a GIFT to mankind!!

Dear Gurlé has thirty-one written letters, which represents *The Proverbs 31* Woman. This book is designed to help women heal from past or current obstacles in their lives. My hope is that each woman reading this book understands that SHE is not alone no matter her background. The letters in my book are speaking about different topics that most women and young ladies have gone through or may have experienced. My prayer is that by the end of this last letter every FEMALE will walk away acknowledging the *Proverbs 31* Woman that she was created and designed to be! But most importantly, my prayer is she will walk away knowing she was NEVER ALONE!

Author's Note

The characters that you will read in each letter of my book are fictional. I did not base any characters from these letters on any personal life experiences of the people I know, know of, or don't know at all. Each character, the stories in each letter, as well as each letter's response, were created and written by me. I wanted to create characters in each letter that feel authentic to situations most women go through in 'real life.' I am certain that every woman and young lady will be able to identify with one or more letters in my book. Letter **8 'Dear Heartbreak'** is the only letter in this book that is based on a true-life experience from one of my past relationships. All other characters in the letters of my book are fictional. This book does contain graphic language when discussing some character's situations and their reactions.

My Prayer for the Reader

Heavenly Father, I come before you asking that you touch each person that is reading this book. I ask that whatever they are in need of that you meet each and every one of those needs. Father, heal them from depression, suicidal thoughts, physical and sexual abuse, loneliness, anxiety and self-hatred and touch them emotionally, spiritually, financially, mentally and physically. Father, whatever is in their way or path that is attempting to block them from their destinies, I ask that you cancel and remove every attack and assignment plotted by the enemy to destroy them and prevent them from getting to their purpose. Father, I ask that you show yourself to each person reading this book and that you move in a divine, miraculous way. Bless them Father, keep their families, children, spouses and loved ones safe from any hurt, harm or danger. I believe by the authority and power of your mighty name that it is done through you.

Amen

About the Author

My birth name is Caprice Williams, but I go by the name Caprice Lamor. I was born at Saint Michaels Hospital in Newark, NJ. I was raised in both Irvington and Newark, New Jersey my entire life. I mostly attended Irvington public schools, but I resided in Newark, New Jersey for most of my life. I graduated from Frank H. Morrell High School in Irvington, New Jersey, formally known as Irvington High School. Growing up, I've always wanted to become a writer. I loved writing poetry, and I always had a great imagination as a child. One day, I was told by a close relative that it was too difficult to become a writer. I was told that I shouldn't pursue writing and should explore other career options because I would never succeed as a writer. I continued to write poetry despite their advice, but I later gave up the will and the desire because I felt discouraged by what was told to me.

I graduated from William Paterson University in Wayne, New Jersey with a degree in communications. After graduation, I worked on call as a Per Diem Teacher with children in grade levels kindergarten through eighth grade in the Newark, East Orange and Orange Public School Systems in New Jersey for three years. I then worked for the state government for thirteen years. I left my job working with the state three weeks before I married my husband, and I relocated from New Jersey to Georgia after we were married. This is when God really began dealing with me on levels that I could never prepare myself for.

I was out of my comfort zone. New Jersey was the only place I had ever known and considered home. After moving to Georgia, I felt lost and I didn't know what to do with myself or my time. From the weather to the people, everything was new and different. I was a city girl. I knew nothing about the country life. During this transition, God showed me that I would go into business for myself. I didn't think that it could happen because I had no resources. I knew very few people, and I had no knowledge of running a business. One day, my husband purchased an art book for me along with colored pencils and markers. He told me to create something. He encouraged me to work on it daily, and he told me that I didn't need anyone to help me but God. He constantly reminded me that God was my one and only source. I played around for months trying to figure out what to create. In Georgia, on July 26, 2016, I created the clothing brand Gurlé, pronounced "Girl." On October 13, 2017 my business website was launched, and my second clothing line and company By' C. Lamor was later created, all thanks to the help and guidance of my heavenly father and my husband, who was my biggest motivator.

The passion to write a book was still burning deep inside of me. After launching my business website, I began to pray to God for more direction. One morning, God awoke me from my sleep. He told me to get a piece of paper and to write down what he was about to tell me. God revealed to me the contents of this book. My husband encouraged me to name my book after my clothing brand. This is how Dear Gurlé was created. After I completed my first book, God revealed to me that I would write my second book for men, called Dear Gurlé, Men Hurt Too.

<u>Contacts/Social Media and Websites:</u>
Website: byclamor.com
Face Book: Gurlé By' C. Lamor
Instagram: @therealcapricelamor @gurleclothingline
@dear_gurle @deargurleletspillowtalk
Twitter: @CapriceLamor

Dedication

I dedicate my book to every little girl, and to every female who has been told,
"No, it's too impossible for you to achieve it." They lied.
-Caprice Lamor-

Acknowledgments

I want to first give honor to my Heavenly Father Jesus Christ for being the head of my life and for being everything to me. Thank you for being my mother, father, sister, brother, but most importantly my confidant when I had no one to turn to when I felt rejected by the people I loved the most. The Lord was there for me during the most difficult and challenging times of my life. I suffered with anxiety, low self-esteem, depression and suicidal thoughts. There was nothing I loved about myself. I thought that everything was wrong with me. But through it all, the Lord assured me every time I felt like giving up that He was there with me. God reminded me that all I had to do is continuously seek him first. My desire to seek God is what saved my life. I owe the Lord every part of my being. Thank you, Lord, for being everything that I need ALL the time.

I want to thank my husband, Prophet Hector Williams. Where do I begin? You came into my life during my most vulnerable and difficult time. I was preparing to go through a terrible separation. I felt broken and defeated. I knew immediately that you were something special. While God used you to help me with my spiritual growth, we also became great friends. I overcame a divorce in 2011, which was one of the hardest things in my life to experience. No one gets married to get a divorce. But who would have known, six years later, you would become more than just my friend? You became my husband, my confidant, my encourager, my teacher, my buddy, my travel partner, but most importantly my prayer partner. I love you deep! Thank you for your support and encouragement. You pushed me to step above my capabilities, and you've always reminded me when I felt defeated that *"Only God Can Do It!"* Thank you for being the man of God that you are. Thank you for representing God inside and outside our home, even when no one else is watching. You are a true leader. I admire and respect you on more levels than you'll ever know.

I want to thank my Mother, Annette Williams, for being the best mother she knew how to be in my life. Thank you for being hard and strict on me, and for giving me tough love. You helped prepare me for the REAL world. I am a strong Woman today, because you never handed me anything. You taught me to go out and get it for myself. I don't rely nor depend on anyone but God this day, because of it. You once told me if I want it, I had to work hard to get it because life was not free. To most people, your tough love may have appeared to be too hard. But I understand why you did what you did and I thank you for it. Love you always.

I want to thank my Grandmother, Eva Bowman, for telling me about God at a very young age. You took me to church every Sunday. I sang in the children's choir and adult choir, I was an usher, and I attended Sunday school and Bible Study. I hated every moment of it. But I thank God for your obedience. You took me no matter what, even if you didn't force anyone else to go. I know and love the Lord the way I do today, because of the seed you planted in me as a child. I remember when I was afraid, you would pray with me at night and you told me God loved me. You taught me my first prayer. You have no idea how much I needed that. You played a vital role in my life and you gave me the emotional support I needed during the most challenging times. God used you to plant His name in me, so I could become who I am today for Him! Thank you, I love you always.

I want to thank all the people in my life that played a supportive role at some point throughout my journey. I want to thank the true, genuine friendships that I've encountered over the years with the few people I know are sincere with their love for me. I also want to thank every person that played a role in my growth. Whether my growth experience with you felt hurtful, malicious, like a betrayal, good or bad, I grew from it. I became a better version of myself, thank you. She still won!

To my most precious godchildren, Paris, Taylor, Sanaii, Tristan and Miles, I am so honored to be called your godmother and to have you in my life. Love you deep!! 💋

—Your God Mom, Caprice

Thirty-One Letters of Content

The end of some response letters includes hotline numbers and resources for help. Anyone who is reading this book or knows someone in need of help can call those numbers for assistance or guidance from any location in the United States.

You are now here in your Cocoon. . .but not for long;

Dear Gurlé,

Being "HER" today is not easy. I don't feel like smiling and pretending to be HER while in school, at work, or around my family, friends, nor my significant other. Little do they know that I'm struggling, struggling to accept the skin that I'm in. With HER, I find myself constantly biting my tongue just to prevent myself from saying what's really on HER mind. If they were able to read HER thoughts - my goodness, she would have no friends in HER life. HER family would look at HER like she's a mean person. And HER significant other would question their relationship. They would only feel this way towards HER because she finally spoke up for HERself and stopped pretending to be HER. I have to dress HER up and make sure HER makeup, HER hair and HER nails are always done. But the funny part is even when I make HER all up, the person inside of HER still doesn't like HER outside. I don't like HER most times. It's hard work trying to be accepted with HER, trying to look the way society wants HER to look. Why can't she just be HERself? She even entertains people she doesn't really care for just to fit in. She's had HER heart broken so many times by the people she trusted the most, but for some odd reason she attracts the same types of people in HER life. She believes in HER dreams, only when she is not sharing them with the people who make HER believe that HER dreams are impossible. They try to convince HER that she should just accept the way HER life is. Oh, she really dislikes those type of people in HER life. They love to speak negatively, and they never have anything positive to say. But despite what they say, she continues to keep those people in HER life. I just want to get today over with, so I can feel better at being HER tomorrow, because today is just not a good day for HER to be myself.

Sincerely, HER

1

Dear HER,

I see that you're having a rough time today being HER. I get it, and I am positive other females may have experienced these same feelings. It requires a lot of dedication to put on a façade every day, and I'm certain it can become very draining after a while. It can also cause you to become resentful towards the people closest to you, that you are pretending to. Why? Because in your heart you want them to recognize and accept YOU. But for some reason in your mind, you believe they understand and like HER much better than they like YOU. Whenever you are being what everyone else wants you to be, instead of being who you desire and need to be for YOU, you are living a lie. Do you know how important it is to be the person who's truly inside of HER? It's crucial to be who you are; if not, many people will miss out on knowing YOU because you continue to be HER. Being YOU is more beneficial than being HER. You don't need HER!! She needs YOU to pretend. So, stop allowing HER to use YOU. I need you to try this exercise when you wake up every morning. Repeat this affirmation to yourself daily, so your day can always begin on a positive note: *"I love YOU. YOU serve a purpose in this life. YOU are strong, beautiful, intelligent and ambitious. YOU deserve happiness and you deserve to be accepted for YOU. This is your life journey; whatever decisions you make will impact YOU more than anyone else's. Stay true to who YOU are. YOU don't need HER to be YOU. Today, will be a great day for me because I've chosen to embrace MYSELF over HER and anyone else."* Every girl should identify her inner power and recognize the special gifts and talents that she carries. And in order for others to see the gifts that you carry, you have to stop hiding yourself inside of HER. Be yourself and let go of the people who are not your real friends. And if anyone decides not to accept YOU for no longer being HER, they never deserved to have YOU in their lives in the first place! I wish you well.

Sincerely, Gurlé

Dear Gurlé,

The Struggle to Love HER is so much harder than you make it sound. I never loved myself. To be quite honest, I've never truly experienced real love. So how could I love myself? I've had some friends and been in some relationships with people who said they loved me, but they all lied to me. I grew up in a home where I watched my mother struggling. My mother and my father never told me that they loved me. I was never told by either parent that I was beautiful. My father was absent most of my life, and my mother was always so angry. I've always felt unwanted by my family. I've never felt that I was truly liked by my peers (*some people are just so superficial*). So, how am I supposed to do this love thing with myself when I constantly feel like I'm battling with myself? I go through so many thoughts in my mind, and most times, I believe what my thoughts are telling me. I don't remember the last time I slept for more than four hours without overthinking my life and who I am supposed to be. I don't know. Maybe you're right, I guess? When I dress HER up every day, it helps me to cover up HER real scars. And she has so many scars that aren't visible to the eyes. I don't know how to help HER. I'm just angry at God for giving me HER life. I struggle with HER and MYSELF every day, and when I go on social media, it looks as if everyone is winning at life. Meanwhile, I'm out here losing. I guess this is why I still pretend to be HER. I'm afraid no one will ever accept the real ME. I'm just mentally drained and tired. Today is another Struggle to Love HER.

Sincerely, The Struggle to Love HER

Dear The Struggle to Love HER,

I understand what you are going through. For a long time in my life, I've struggled with not feeling loved by my parents, family and even my friends. It mattered to me what people thought about me, too. And I searched for love my entire life. You are not alone with the struggle to love HER. I get why some parents are unable to demonstrate love to their children. Most times, parents are still dealing with hurt and abandonment issues from their childhood. Some parents only know how to love as much as they were given love. But every day, when you look at yourself, remember that you do matter. Unfortunately, we live in a world filled with hurt and damaged people. But you have to fight to cure yourself with self-love before you can expect to be loved by anyone else. You must learn to love, clap and cheer for the parts of your existence that no one will ever clap for. When you love yourself and embrace every scar, the people around you have no other choice but to love you and accept your scars, too. The Struggle to Love HER, you will know and experience how it feels to receive genuine love one day. There are people in this world who are waiting to cross paths with you because they need the love that's inside of you, and you need the love that's inside of them. It is destined for each person's life to experience one of the most precious gifts that was granted to us, which is LOVE. But I need you to start with you first – receive you, accept you and grow in love with you. Oh, and as for social media, do not measure yourself up against or base someone else's happiness on your life. Yes, there are people whose lives are going the way their posts are reflecting on Instagram, Facebook and Twitter. But you also have a lot of people who are not posting the truth about their lives. Regardless of if what they are posting is true or not, you cannot get yourself caught up in what you think someone else is getting or if they have more than you or not. Stay focused on LEARNING to LOVE YOU! Best wishes, always.

Sincerely, Gurlé

Dear Gurlé,

Looking for Acceptance is all I have been doing my entire life. I've always done things to be accepted by people, especially men. When those feelings and actions aren't reciprocated back to me, I feel used. But why should I feel used when I'm bringing this on myself? I have done some things that I am too ashamed to tell God about, yet alone you. I became promiscuous at a very young age. I developed a bad reputation with the guys around my neighborhood, which stands to this day. When I was younger, I was never considered pretty or popular, but I've always had the desire to fit in. When I had sex with boys when I was younger, I only did it to be accepted by them. I really believed that they liked me. I was gullible. I allowed my friends to encourage me to be promiscuous because they were, too. I wanted people to see me as being down to earth and cool. I'm not the most attractive girl, but I've always been told that I have the perfect body, which has always made me feel good about myself. I even smoked marijuana just to fit in, and today, it's become a bad habit that I've brought into my adult life. Now, I need to smoke all the time, especially if I'm feeling stressed. I'm currently thirty-five years old. I've had two surgeries, one surgery to enlarge my breast size and the second surgery to alter my face. Today, I get all the attention I need from men every day, and at one point it felt good. Now I'm beginning to feel unhappy with myself. I look at myself in the mirror, and I don't recognize me. What have I become just to be accepted? I am currently in a one-year relationship with a married man, who loves and accepts me. He's in a fifteen-year marriage, and although he tells me every day that he is getting a divorce, I know he will never leave his wife for me. He says he'll leave her after each time we make passionate love in our secret hotel spot where we meet two to three times per week in suite 503. But deep in my heart, I've always known that if he was leaving his wife,

5

he would have left her by now. His wife is so plain. She doesn't wear the latest fashions, and her hair is always pulled back. She is what you would consider a "Plain Jane." Oh yes, I met his wife before I met him. She is a sweet lady. Once, he took me to their home when his wife was out of town with their two children, and he fucked me in their bed and on top of their kitchen counter. I didn't feel any remorse about it at all because I believed him when he told me that he loved me every time he made love to me. I believed him when he told me that he wanted me to be the mother to his children. I'm now at a place in my life where I want more. I want my own husband, and I want to go back to college to complete my degree in education. If only I could get past the need to feel accepted and stop seeking attention that is not always good. How can I learn to accept myself after all I've done? I am in a relationship with a married man. As of this day, I have a bad reputation, and I am still seen as the woman who breaks apart the happy home. I feel so lost, and I am ready to get my life together. Is it too late at thirty-five years old, after all I've done? Karma does exist, and I will never want what I've done towards another woman to come back to me. Will I ever be accepted by the right man with the right love? I'm tired of Looking for Acceptance. I am ready to be accepted genuinely and naturally for me. I am ready to become a new me.

Sincerely, Looking for Acceptance

Dear Looking for Acceptance,

I want to first thank you for being so transparent. That was very bold, honest and brave of you to share your story. Please understand, this is a no judgement zone. But before I begin, just know that you are STILL worth it. I believe that most girls and women can relate to "Looking for Acceptance." This is something that a lot of us have searched for during some period of our lives. You've explained that you became promiscuous at a young age and that you never felt pretty or popular. Your body was the one thing that received the most attention and acceptance from guys. And as you became older in age, you enhanced the one thing (*your body*) that you felt gave you the acceptance you've always desired. Wanting acceptance is another way of saying looking for **LOVE**, because most people believe being accepted means being loved. The one person you needed to accept you the most was YOU. It's never been about the guys or how you looked to others. It's always been about how you felt about yourself. You did the things you've done to make you feel validated or loved because you didn't believe you were already enough. But YOU were always more than enough! You had surgery on your body to maintain your own reality of what you thought it took to be accepted by men. The married man you're having an affair with *is not your boyfriend - he is someone else's husband*. His wife is considered a "Plain Jane" to you, but you have to look at it like this, he accepted his wife with all of her "Plain" ways because he married her. We can agree that most men are visual. But not every man is just looking for a woman's outside beauty. He's looking for her inside beauty as well. When a man truly wants to be with you, he will give all of his time and dedication to building a relationship with you. You would NOT be kept a secret. He would make your identity and role in his life known to the people that are most important in his life, as well as in your life. If the married man truly LOVED and RESPECTED you, he would have ended his marriage with his wife the correct way, before having any further involvement with you. Then once his marriage was completely dissolved, he would have approached you the appropriate way. I need you to understand that when YOU accept YOU, everyone else around you will have no other choice but to accept you, too. No, he will never leave his wife for you. Please understand that life, love, acceptance and happiness are never too late for you. But first, you have to end this affair with the married man. Second, you have to stop allowing your past to hold you hostage. Who you were at a younger age is NOT who you have to continue being. LET HER GO! Your past and other people's opinions of who you once were are no longer your business! Third, you need to take time for YOU; get to know yourself on the inside. You've spent enough time focused on the outside. Fourth, go back to school if that's your heart's desire. It's never too late. Fifth, start learning to ACCEPT you, and when you meet new people in your life, be yourself - nothing more, nothing less. The ones that are true will show themselves to be real and consistent in your life. And last, YOU ARE STILL WORTH IT!

Sincerely, Gurlé

"People treat you the way you treat yourself. Learn to be your first love."

-Caprice Lamor-

Dear Gurlé,

Secret Depression is something that I've been secretly battling with for some time. The funny part is that everyone looks to me as if I'm unbreakable. I'm always told how much I'm admired by so many ladies and how they wish they had the positive outlook on life the way that I do. I am the go-to person for everything. Just call me the relationship expert. Yet, I am divorced, currently single and horny as hell! That's another discussion we will have later. Everyone expects me to remain strong even through my biggest battles. I never get any sympathy or empathy when I have a major crisis in my life. I'm supposed to just put on my big girl hat and cape and handle it like I am Wonder Woman. When I was married, my ex-husband comforted the other woman when she and I both learned together that he was cheating on me with her. Apparently, he lied to her about his relationship status. According to his profile on the dating site, he was a "single male." He was more concerned about the other woman's feelings over mine. When I later confronted him about it, he told me that he knew that I was a strong woman and could handle anything. He told me that the other woman was weak, and she would try and do something crazy, such as harm herself. I guess I do appear to be the strongest and happiest person on the planet. You should see me. I promise, I could win an Oscar for best supporting actress. I'm well put together. My hair and nails are always done. I wear the best quality fashions and hell you ought to see my condo! I drive a Mercedes Benz truck, and I make a six-figure salary. I do very well financially for myself. Oh, and I have no children. That would be considered a plus. This explains why I am so strong and have so much time to heal other people's lives when my life is secretly falling apart. Okay, I'm being facetious right now. But you get my drift. One day, I had the worst panic attack of my life. I thought that I was going to die. I woke up gasping for air, unable to

11

breathe. I couldn't understand what was happening to me. Since that day two years ago, I have been very depressed. There were times I've slept all day and didn't take phone calls from anyone. Because my life is viewed as being so extravagant, no one ever noticed that I was going through anything. They assumed that I was living my life as I've always pretended to be. There was one period of time when I didn't shower for three days, and I am a germophobe!!! I didn't shave any parts of my body, and I ate ice cream and potato chips for breakfast, lunch and dinner. When it was time for me to return back to my "life", I put on my Oscar-award-winning face and played the role as I have played it these past two years. Today, I am tired. I am worn. I am frightened. I am uncertain. I am empty, and I need someone to encourage ME and tell ME that everything is going to be okay. I need someone to have sympathy for ME and empathize with my pain. I need someone to ask me, *"Are you okay?"* I need to be vulnerable without judgement. No, I have no desire to harm myself at all. Not everyone who's depressed has suicidal thoughts. Today, I am just reaching out for help.

Sincerely, Secret Depression

Dear Secret Depression,

Thank you for reaching out for help. There are so many women in this world like you who are feeling overwhelmed, defeated, overlooked, and they are battling with secret depression as well. They wake up every day with an agenda to save everyone in the world, except themselves. The sad part is depression can go unnoticed by the people we love and surround ourselves with most often. There are people walking around every day that are one second away from having a nervous breakdown. Unfortunately, we cannot identify depression in everyone. However, there are some people who can be identified with depression, because they are giving the signs and indications in their appearances, behaviors and even their conversations. But then you have people like yourself who are well put together, always appearing to be happy and appearing to have it all together, yet are dealing with depression, too. First, I want to start off by saying that YOU ARE NOT ALONE. The fact that you've acknowledged there is a mental issue with you is very brave of you. People don't realize that depression is part of having a mental issue, such as worry, stress, and anxiety. It doesn't mean that you are crazy; it just means that some people have more difficulty coping with daily life issues more than others. You've made the first step by admitting it. The next step that you need to take is to seek counseling from a therapist, psychologist and/ or spiritual guidance from a pastor to better understand where the depression comes from. I know that a lot of people don't agree with seeing a therapist or a psychologist because they feel they would be labeled as being crazy. But you're not crazy. Sometimes we need someone to talk to that doesn't know anything about us and who won't judge us. It's helpful to let out your feelings in a place where it's confidential and professional. I recognize that most people dislike discussing their past, especially when it has caused them a great deal of pain. However, the past is what caused a lot of people to create and accept unhealthy friendships and relationships with people as well as unhealthy relationship with themselves. Sometimes we have to go back to the broken pieces that we left hidden under a rug, so we can get rid of those pieces for good. And not everyone may be suffering from depression due to past hurt or past experiences. It could be things that they are currently dealing with right now, such as a recent medical diagnosis, the loss of a job, or loved one, a divorce, a troublesome relationship, family problems, or a close friendship that ended, or the recent birth of a child (postpartum). There are some that may be dealing with a mental health issue, such as being bipolar, that may be triggering the depression that they have no idea is a family trait. Despite everything, there is help for everyone that is dealing with depression. Please seek professional counseling and help. One thing you need to do is confide with a close friend or family member that you trust about your struggles. You need all the support that you can get. Please stay encouraged and know that there is hope. You will get through this. Below I have attached 24-hour depression hotlines for you or anyone else that you know may be suffering with depression. Please reach out to someone. I hope all works out for you.

Sincerely, Gurlé

National Hopeline Network: This 24-hour depression hotline is for people who are depressed and thinking about suicide. When you call 1-800-442-HOPE (4673), you will be connected with a crisis hotline volunteer.

Postpartum Support International: If you or someone you know is experiencing postpartum depression, call 1-800-944-4773, e-mail support@postpartum.net, or visit postpartum.net for resources and information.

National Suicide Prevention Lifeline: If you are experiencing distress, tell someone you trust and call 1-800-273-TALK (8253) or text "BRAVE" to 731731.

Dear Gurlé,

I am a forty-year-old *Childless Mother.* I've never had children and NO! I've never had an abortion. NO! Nothing is wrong with my body! And NO! I've never had any miscarriages. I just want to make that clear. It just never happened, that's all. I've never gotten pregnant before in my life, and that's been fine with me. Hey, no children. Life is good. I am free to come and go as I please. I was raised in a family with all women, no men. I've always had to see about my younger siblings. My great aunt made my cousins and I believe that having children was the worst thing to do. So, we all excelled with high achievements in school as well as in our careers. We all live successful lives, and none of us have children. I'm not married yet. But I am currently dating a guy who I like a lot. The issues that I am experiencing now are with my family, friends and my coworkers. I am so tired of people making me feel LESS THAN A WOMAN just because I don't have any children. My friends who recently became new mothers (*the same ones who once before felt my pain*) are making me feel badly about it, too. All I ever hear my friends talk about anymore are their children, children's fathers or their husbands. It just makes me want to go and throw a pity party for myself. I just sit there while they all engage in exchanging children's notes that I cannot relate to. My family is no better. Now, all of a sudden, they want me to have a lot of children. All I hear from my family is, *"What are you waiting for? Your eggs are getting low, and you're getting older."* Mother's Day is the worst! They love to say to me *"Aww you're still considered a mother, too, even though you don't have children of your own. You have helped care for other people's children."* It's so depressing. I know that I'm not anyone's mother. And I'm okay with it. I don't need to be reminded. At my workplace it's another story. Every other day someone is rubbing or touching my stomach saying, *"You're next"* after another coworker announces

15

their pregnancy to the office staff. As if a baby and a husband will magically appear in my life. My coworkers also believe that because I don't have children or a husband to go home to after work, I can work late hours every night and do their jobs as well. They also believe that I should trade my holiday vacation times with them, too, since they are the ones with the family and not me. I am also tired of people assuming that because I am single with no children or a spouse that I am RICH. I still have bills to pay as well. I constantly hear, "*Oh you don't have any children, so you should have money.*" News Flash!! Single people get taxed the hardest! I am not RICH, and I still have responsibilities just like they do. Sorry if my words sound like I am screaming at you. The truth is, at this point in my life, I don't want any children. I am truly tired of people making me feel bad about my personal decision not to have children. I don't want to have children now, especially at this age in my life. Although I know that it's possible for me to have children at my age, I just have no desires to do so. There were times I could admit that I had "Baby Fever," and I wanted to have children. Unfortunately, I couldn't start a family without a husband. I just want people to leave me alone about my personal decision. And I want to be able to hang out with my friends without hearing them talk about their children all night long. I don't mind the conversation for a while, but not all night long. And if I see one more baby picture, I will scream. I get it. Every mother feels that their child is the cutest, and I agree, all children are **ABSOLUTELY BEAUTIFUL**. But I don't want to look at pictures or hear about children all the time. I hope I'm not coming off as a mean person. I'm just speaking from a female's perspective who is NOT a MOTHER. I do have godchildren and younger family members that I've nurtured and given motherly love to throughout the years. That should count for something, right? The world needs to know that just because a female doesn't have a child, it doesn't make her LESS OF A WOMAN or make her a SELFISH WOMAN. There are females who have children,

16

but they are not fit nor qualified to be mothers, and they are the ones that are very selfish. Also, just because I don't have children, it does not mean that I am incapable of giving a mother advice concerning her children. I may not understand how it felt to carry a child or to go through long hours of labor, but I understand what it's like to be a human and to have feelings. I just wanted to write to you to express my feelings. I must admit that this mother issue bothers me. Please tell me if I am being insensitive towards my friends who are new mothers and other mothers out in the world. I just need them to also be sensitive towards my feelings and the feelings of women all around the world who have made the personal choice to be Childless Mothers.

Sincerely, Childless Mother

Dear Childless Mother,

Thank you for reaching out and for sharing your experiences. I truly believe that there are other women in this world who feel exactly how you are feeling. You were just bold enough to say it! You are not wrong for how you are feeling. I have heard many childless mothers say that as soon as other women that are mothers learned that they didn't have children, they treated them differently. I must admit that motherhood is a beautiful gift that was given to us by God. There is nothing wrong with having children. Children are also a gift from God. Unfortunately, we have some people in the world who are insensitive to women who are childless mothers. There are women in this world who desperately want to become a mother. But because of their medical issues, they have a hard time conceiving or carrying a child to full term. There are also women in this world that had a bad experience. They were raped or something happened to them at birth as a child that made their chances of becoming a mother impossible. Then there are women who are single and perfectly healthy, and they want to have children one day soon. They're just waiting and hoping that their husband will show up, so they can have the *"American Dream"* after all – the white picket fence, children and a dog. We also have women like you, who made the choice to not have children after a certain age or at all. People should be more sensitive about this topic because you never know why a woman doesn't have children of her own. And it's not anyone's business to know. Also, I've never agreed with any person rubbing on a pregnant woman's belly. So, it's even more inappropriate to rub a woman's belly who's not pregnant. People really need to learn about personal space. Regarding your friends, it's okay for you to have your personal feelings. But remember that motherhood is new and exciting for them. Allow them to have their moments and to share their happiness with you because you would want the same from them as well.

18

What I recommend you should do, whenever you feel you need an emotional break or a little balance in your life, is surround yourself with other woman who don't have children. I can see that it bothers you because you're feeling that you can no longer relate to your friends and that you share nothing else in common. You feel that you're losing touch with them. I promise you they will NEED you down the road. You will become their sound ear when they are in need of emotional breaks from their children and spouses. In life, we all go through different experiences. But in the end, real friendships will stand the test of time. As far as your coworkers, remind them when they get a little too close in your personal space. And keep your work relationships, work related only. Regarding family, LOL. Family will always be family. Unfortunately, we all have experienced being the topic of holiday and family gatherings. Some things will never change. Just learn how to duck and dodge the uncomfortable family topics. I hope everything works out for you.

Childless Mothers Matter, Too!

Sincerely, Gurlé

Dear Gurlé,

Ms. Independent is my name, and I wear it proudly! I am constantly told by others that my standards are way too high. I was raised by both of my parents. My parents are legally married. They've been married for thirty years. After my father cheated on my mother with my mother's first cousin, my mother kicked my father out of their home. Apparently, my father was having an affair with my mother's first cousin for as long as they had been married. My mother caught them together in our basement having sex. We were having a Fourth of July family barbeque at the time it happened. The music was loud, and the house was filled with family and friends. We were all having a good time. My father and my mother's cousin went missing for a little too long. My mother was beginning to suspect something was going on, so she went to look for them and found them together. I was ten at the time. My mother and father never divorced. My father is currently in an open relationship with my mother's first cousin, whom he's cheated with all of these years. It's so weird, because my family behaves as if it's okay whenever they show up together at our family gatherings as a couple. Everyone is fully aware that my father is still legally married to my mother. I still attend family gatherings, but my mother stays home. She is very angry and bitter with my father. I still love my father despite what he's done, but I've lost respect for him. My mother on the other hand, is in a relationship with a man who's always liked her since they were younger. He worships the ground my mother walks on, but my mother is only with him because he has money. She needs him to help her with the house mortgage and other bills. My mother only received a high school education, so finding a decent job was always difficult for her. She worked at the high school cafeteria for years. I've watched my mother give herself to a man that she doesn't love just to receive financial help. I promised myself when I was ten that when I became older, I would never allow a man to have that much power over me. So, this is why I am Ms. Independent, and I don't rely on a man for anything. I have a job making six figures. I have my master's degree, and I am currently working on my Ph.D. I am also a homeowner. NO man has helped me accumulate the things that I have today. It was all me, and I am proud of myself. I don't respect men who live off of women or who don't take care of their responsibilities. I don't have time for men with children. If he's not making six figures or more, or ready to travel the world, then we definitely have nothing to talk about. This is what I've always felt strongly in my heart. I am about to turn forty in a couple of months, and I am still single, and I have yet to find that man who fits all my criteria. My girlfriend is a lawyer and her husband works as a school teacher. He had two children prior to their marriage. She had no children, and she is happily married and in love. They are expecting their first child together this month. I must admit that I feel a little jealous. I just cannot seem to get over my list of how my husband is supposed to look, how tall he is supposed to be, if he has a beard, muscles and a college degree, no children and on and on. I went to a women's seminar three years ago. They said to write down on a piece of paper exactly how we want our husband to look down to his height, to write down the qualities and the education we want him to possess. I did all of that, and I'm still attracting the total opposite of what I wrote on my list. Well, I must be honest with you about something. There is this guy who has asked me on a date several times, but I declined. He recently sent me flowers asking me out again. He told me in the note if I turned him down again, he would leave me alone. But he had to try once more. He's really not my type at all. He's very cute. He's roughly my height, just a few inches taller. So, if I wore my heals, we could look each other eye to eye. His style of clothing is a little corny for me. He works for a construction company. He has no college degree. He's never been married, and he doesn't

21

have any children. I must admit, he really is a nice guy. One day, he was wearing a t-shirt, and I couldn't believe how fit his body looked. I was impressed. But I kept telling myself that he cannot be the one, because he doesn't fit the list I wrote down three years ago. This is what I told myself over and over again. I don't know what to do. I am asking you for your advice because I've been told that you are the person to contact for things like this. Should I go out with him or wait for the guy that I described on my list three years ago?

Sincerely, Ms. Independent

Dear Ms. Independent,

Hello, and thank you for reaching out to me. Wow. I can definitely understand how and why you have developed this "Ms. Independent" attitude. First of all, your father cheated on your mother. You had to watch your mother depend on a man that she didn't love to financially help her. The one man and first love of your life, your father, left his family financially struggling. He failed you. He didn't fight for his marriage after thirty years. And now he's parading around the family with his mistress, your mother's first cousin, his now "current" girlfriend. Your mother is now bitter and angry and using someone who truly loves her the same way that she was used by your father. So, I get it. It is justified why you developed this attitude. But you are not your parents. That was a decision your parents made in their marriage. Your father's infidelity was wrong, and your mother was also wrong. She used a person who truly loved her for his finances. Therefore, you promised yourself that you would become successful so you would never have to depend on any man for help. I need you to understand that there is nothing wrong with accepting help from a man that loves you and whose goal is to become your husband. It doesn't make you less independent because he may assist you in any financial way. There is also nothing wrong with wanting to live an independent life. But when you desire to have a companion, or a husband in your life, you cannot have that attitude. Yes, it is true. There are some men out in the world that don't believe in financially helping their female partners, especially if he is not legally married to her. You also have some married men who believe in going half on all household bills and other married men who believe that it's the male's responsibility to handle all the household bills in the home. There are also some men who are okay with their wives or mates carrying the full financial load

23

in their home. But if those partners in those particular cases are okay with however their home is set up, then that's their personal business. However, I'm almost positive that there aren't too many women that want a man who is cheap and not willing to support her if they are together, especially in marriage. But it all boils down to a person's morals and values. One thing I know for sure is that you cannot live your life according to the outcome of your parent's marriage. You met a guy who sounds like a good catch. But because he doesn't fit all of the qualities you wrote down on a list three years ago you pass him over. My grandmother once told me, *"It's not how the package looks. It's what's inside the package that matters most."* In life, good, decent women miss out on the greatest men, because he's not tall enough. He doesn't make that much money. He doesn't have a beard or he's too corny. But most women overlook the fact that he opens and closes her doors. He's not religious, but he's faithful and has a close relationship with God. There is nothing wrong with being "Ms. Independent" if you choose to never commit or get married to anyone. But one thing I've learned in life is that as you grow older in age, what a person has is not going to matter to you. What will matter is what's in their heart. I've heard my single friends say, *"Oh I have to be attracted to the person that I'm with."* As you begin to know a person, you start noticing how pretty their teeth are, how they give you butterflies just the way that they look at you. You also notice how caring they are towards you. You begin to notice more things that you didn't have on your check list. The next thing you know, you're falling in love with what you see on their inside, and you become more attracted to their outside. Give the guy a chance. Tell him that you will go out on a date with him and see what happens. He may just enhance your list. Let me know what happens later. I wish you the best of happiness.

Sincerely, Gurlé

Dear Gurlé,

Ms. Independent is now Ms. Relationship! You were so right about the advice that you gave me. I must admit that it took me two weeks to answer him back after you responded to my letter four months ago. I called him, and I agreed to go out on a date with him. We arranged to go out on a date one week after we spoke. I didn't want him to know where I lived just yet, so I agreed to meet him at my job parking lot where we initially first met. One day, he was doing construction on my work building, and when he saw me, he introduced himself to me. Back to the date, we agreed to meet at six thirty in the evening on a Thursday. The evening was beautiful. It was seventy-eight degrees outside with a cool breeze. He arrived in a two-seater black Porsche. I was like *"Okay!"* I was totally not expecting that to happen. I never saw the type of vehicle that he drove. I guess it's because I wasn't interested at that time. When he walked from his vehicle, he was wearing a pair of dark khaki pants, a button-down short-sleeve shirt and very nice casual shoes. He smelled so good! I had to double look to see if he was the same guy. I played it cool. He greeted me by kissing the back of my right hand. He stated that he had a nice evening planned for us, and he asked me if I'd feel comfortable riding in his vehicle or would I feel better following him to the destination. I agreed to ride with him. As we walked towards his vehicle, he opened and closed my door for me, so far so good. We arrived at our location about thirty minutes later. He took me to this really nice restaurant which served the absolute BEST salmon I've ever had in my life! Everything was good and fresh. I noticed during our time at dinner how the waiters were very attentive to us. We didn't have to wait long for service at all. I was beyond impressed. We had a great conversation, and we laughed a lot. He has a great sense of humor, not too much but just right. He is a very intelligent man. He disclosed to me during dinner that he has a very close relationship with his mother. He is an only child, he's forty-four years old and his sign is Sagittarius. I've never dated a Sagittarius before. We talked for hours at the dinner table and time began to pass. It was near nine o'clock when we finished dinner. As we were leaving the restaurant, I told him how nice the staff was to us and how I wanted to give them a good rating. I am good for reporting restaurants, good or bad. My girlfriends hate going out to eat with me because I am a perfectionist, and I always expect "A Plus" service. He smiled and said to me, he would tell the owner personally, because they knew each other very well. I thought, now I see why we received the star treatment. Next, he took me to listen to some jazz music. It was a very nice outdoor venue overlooking the water. It was absolutely relaxing and mellow. We left around eleven to head back to my work place so I could retrieve my vehicle. After we arrived back to my work place, he told me that the owner was very happy that I was pleased with the service at the restaurant tonight. I said to him, "*I never saw you make a phone call to anyone.*" He confessed to me that he was the owner of the restaurant. I just sat there in disbelief. He explained to me that he owns the construction company that works on my job building, and the restaurant we just left, he built it with his bare hands. I was already blown away by his charm and how gentle and attentive he was towards me, but to discover that he is a self-built entrepreneur. All I thought about in that moment was you and how you told me to overlook the exterior and to get to know him on the inside. I judged him because he didn't have a college degree, and there he was with several successful businesses. We have been seeing each other for the past three months, and as of last week, we made it official. I am finally off the market. We have not engaged in sex, as of yet. We are taking our time. We want to get to know each other more. We are going with the flow. But he sure is the BEST kisser! Thank you so much for everything! And your grandmother was right! "*It's not how the package looks. It what's inside that matters most.*"

Sincerely, Ms. Independent

Dear Gurlé,

I Like People, But I Don't Like Being Around People.
I know this may sound very strange to you, but it's true on my
part. I am one of the nicest people on the planet, but I don't like
being around people all of the time. Some may consider it to be
shade. But it's not shade at all. I'm the type of person that goes to
work and to the gym, makes a stop at the store for dinner, then
goes home and puts on their pajamas. I am usually showered and
in my pjs no later than 8pm every night, including weekends. I sit
in front of the television with my glass of wine and snacks, and I
binge watch all of my favorite television shows while I periodically
check my social media and send certain unwanted calls to my
voicemail. There are only a couple of people whose phone calls
I usually take. I just don't want to be bothered. You would look
at me and think that my life is exciting. It could be exciting, but
I just choose to live my life as a loner. I get invited to everyone's
functions, and at the initial invitation my plan is to attend, but as
soon as the date grows closer, I dread the fact that I may have to be
in attendance with folks that I know, I hardly know, or don't care
to know at all. When an event that I was invited to gets canceled,
I pretend that I'm saddened, but I am the happiest person in the
world. As shady as this may sound, if I'm not invited to any of my
friends' events, I feel some type of way. One of my girlfriends told
me that she didn't invite me to one particular function because I
never show up to any events when she does invite me. The nerve
of her to make the decision for me! Although, she is correct; nine
times out of ten I would have canceled. But I still want to get
invited. Now don't get me wrong – when I do decide to come out,
they cannot handle all of this perfection, honey. I come correct
from head to toe. Then they say to me *"Girl you're too much."*
But in a good way. There are times I do show up, and no one ever
knows that I am there, except the persons who invited me. I do

this because I like to sit back and observe people. You'll learn a lot this way, and it's good to not always be seen or heard sometimes. I am the same way with my family. If I could keep away from them, I would. I'm learning that just because you're related to someone doesn't mean that you have to like them. I have a few relatives that if I saw them in the streets, I would consider them to be my enemy. I'm just keeping it real with you. But despite everything, I am really a nice person, and when I love someone, I love them genuinely. I'm beginning to recognize that some of my closest friends are taking me the wrong way, like when they call me, and I don't respond. Then moments later they'll see me post on my social media pages, and then they'll write a comment under the post I just posted saying, *"I just called you."* There are also those who feel that every time they invite me somewhere, I never show up, and if I do, I'm usually the first person to leave early. I am the QUEEN of having an imaginary to-do list just so I have a reason to not be around people too long. But just because I am this way it doesn't make me a mean person. I do like people, but I just don't like being around people all the time. Is there a way that I can make the people who matter in my life know that I do care for them? What can I do to make them feel that I am available for them, while still being loyal to who I am as a person? I don't want the invites or the phone calls to stop. But I need them to understand that this is also me. Can you give me some advice on how to better approach the people who matter most in my life?

Sincerely, I Like People, But I Don't Like Being Around People

Dear I Like People, But I Don't Like Being Around People,

I know a lot of women who can definitely relate to you. There are a lot of people who feel this exact way. There's really not an explanation. This is just people's personalities. You want to be involved in your friend's lives, but on your time. Is it wrong? Yes and no. It's not wrong because you have the right to be who you are and a right to give your time to those that you choose to. It's also not right because on the other hand, what if your friend really needs you, but because you never make yourself available, they can't call on you. We all have responsibilities to the people whose lives we choose to be a part of. There are times that we may have to support a friend, or even a family member, when we are tired and don't feel like being bothered. It's important because you never know when your turn will come one day, or when you will need someone to answer your phone call or to show up for your special event. This is part of having relationships with the people we love. Regarding family, I can definitely understand. Just because you are related to someone doesn't mean that you have to like them as a person. That's very true. But respect will always be important on both sides no matter what. You may not have to like them, and they may not like you, but you must respect one another. This is with any relationships. It's also a form of respect when you answer your friend's phone call or show up to an event that's important to them. No, you shouldn't have to attend every function to prove that you are someone's friend. Just show up for the most important ones. If you sit down with the friends who matter most to you and are just completely honest about how you enjoy your days when you're alone, I'm sure that they will understand. But if you continue not showing up and leaving before the party really begins, you will lose out on the friends who matter the most to you. I'm not suggesting that you stop being who you are, but I am suggesting that you show up as much as you can, rather than less than you're willing to. I believe that you are a genuinely loving person. And I strongly believe that your friends already know this about you. They may understand you better than you think. But that doesn't mean that it may not hurt their feelings at times. Just talk to them, and tell them that you'll do better. I believe that everything will work out for you. Thank you so much for sharing your story. It's a REAL blessing to be invited anywhere or to have any friends at all. You are blessed.

Sincerely, Gurlé

Dear Gurlé,

This is the worst *Heartbreak* I've ever felt in my entire life. I was in a relationship with my first love since we were teenagers. He was the first guy that I've ever loved. We were "The Couple" in high school. He was very popular in school, too. He was tall and extremely handsome. He also played on the football team his freshmen year. All the girls wanted to be with him, but I was never worried about the other girls. Afterall, he had liked and pursued me since the eighth grade. I remember during our eighth-grade gym class, I fell and sprained my ankle playing volleyball. He carried me all the way to the nurse's office. It was the funniest thing to me. He once told me that he brought candy to class every day just to share it with me. Before high school, though I thought he was handsome, I was never interested in dating him. We graduated from junior high school and entered our freshmen year at the high school. I ended up dating one of his friend's early freshmen year, but it didn't last long at all. I still never saw myself being in a relationship with him. One day, towards the end of our freshmen year, our classmate convinced me to give him a chance. We exchanged numbers, and we talked all throughout the summer over the telephone, and we fell in love. We dated from freshmen to junior year in high school. I would never forget the day that he broke up with me, October 11, 1991. He told me that he needed his space. I was devastated and broken. It was hard seeing him in school every day in between classes after our break-up. He looked happy without me. I had meltdowns during the school hours, and I often heard rumors that he was seeing other girls. Eventually, he stopped attending school altogether, and I didn't see him as much. A year went by after our breakup, and I couldn't get him off of my mind. I was still in love with him. By that time, he was in a new relationship with an underclassman from our high school. She was pretty, but I knew that it wouldn't last. I

31

knew deep down he still loved me. But I eventually moved on the best way that I could. I graduated high school, and I went onto college. I dated someone for a short period of time, but my first love would never leave my heart. When I was twenty years old, I received a call from him. It was like a scene from a movie. When I heard his voice on the other end of the telephone, I thought that I was dreaming. *"How did he track me down?"* I thought to myself. I learned during his phone call that he called my mother's home and obtained my information. He confessed his love to me that day. He told me that he never stopped loving me and that I was always the one for him. He asked if he could come and see me, and we agreed to meet that night. When I saw him for the first time in three years, all of my feelings for him came rushing back to my heart at once, but I didn't show it. We sat down to talk. He poured his heart out to me. But I didn't make it easy for him. I told him how badly he hurt me in the past. He apologized and I believed him. I felt that we were meant to be because he came back for me. Like the saying goes *"If you love something set it free. If it comes back, it's yours. If not, it wasn't meant to be."* That night we kissed, and we officially got back together. Today, I am twenty-eight years old. We remained together throughout these years, but we were having a lot of issues. We lived together for a while before I decided to move out. I couldn't take the infidelity anymore. There were so many girls. He didn't know that I had his password to his home voicemail. I heard all of the voice messages left by other females. It broke my heart. He once dated his best friend's (*at that time*) sister, while we were in a relationship together. I was there for this man during his biggest ups and his lowest downs. I couldn't understand how he could continuously hurt me. But for whatever reason, I couldn't let him go, no matter how many times he cheated on me. I loved him. I wanted to become his wife one day. I felt that I deserved to carry his last name because I had endured and invested so much into our relationship. We had been together for eight years when I was told some devastating news by my relative. During one of our many on and off again breakups, I learned that he was engaged to be married. I just knew there was some kind of confusion because we were only broken up for a couple of weeks, and I never considered it a real breakup. This was very common for us to break up one week and be back together the following week. The people that personally knew us never considered us to be broken apart because even during our breakups we were together. We still were together sexually as well. After my relative told me, I immediately called him. When he answered his telephone, I knew another woman was present with him just by the way he verbally spoke to me. It was a different tone. He spoke as if I was just a girl that he dated for a short period of time. He told me that he wished me the best in my life. He expressed that he was moving forward without me, in so many words. But he never shared that he was engaged or in a relationship with another person. I didn't believe him. I knew him better than he knew himself. He loved me. He was trying to impress this woman or whomever she was to him. I thought to myself, *"this chick must have money"* because he was all about being rich and living in a big mansion someday. I recall the days when he and I would ride around the rich neighborhoods, imagining that it will be us living that way one day, too. I allowed him to talk and put on a show for this woman that I knew was there. I could have said a lot to make her question his character. But I chose to just listen. After we disconnected, I cried until no more tears could fall. I learned from his sister, who I had a very close relationship with, that it was true. He was marrying this young lady that he had met less than a year prior. All I could think is that I gave this man my ENTIRE life. What was I going to do without him? Well, he married her, and they later had a child together. Now I sit here at twenty-nine years old. I have no idea what I am going to do with this broken heart of mine. He called and told me that he loved me even after he married her. He told me that I was still the one, even after he married her. But I am still alone and heartbroken. How could I ever love again? I was supposed to have been his wife, right? I am destroyed, and I need to know how to heal from this. I gave this man my heart for over fifteen years of my life. I know this may sound crazy, but I know that he loves me, and he has never stopped loving me to this day. Please help me mend my broken heart, so that I can one day love again.

Sincerely, Heartbreak 💔

Dear Heartbreak,

Thank you for being vulnerable and open with your heart. I know too well what a heartbreak feels like. I am truly sorry that you had to endure the pain of watching the love of your life marry someone else. I was hoping that your story had a happier ending. The best advice that I can give to you right now is to take time for you. You have spent the majority of your life loving and waiting for a man who clearly couldn't love you the way that you deserved. I will not promise you that this healing process will be easy. But I promise you that when you come out of this healing phase, you're going to be much stronger and wiser. I don't know why our hearts won't do what our minds tell them to do. We cannot help nor control who we love. But we can control how we move forward in these hurtful situations. I do believe that he loved you, but he was selfish and about himself. One day, he will wake up and realize that he had the perfect person in his life, and he can never have her back again. You have to let go and move on. Do not answer his phone calls or agree to see him for sexual favors because he is a MARRIED MAN. He will definitely try to reach you because you guys have such a strong history together, and your love is very familiar to him. You don't need to date anyone right now because you are very vulnerable. You will only cause more hurt to yourself. Give yourself at least a year to recover, and then slowly get back into the dating scene. One thing I want you to know, because most women blame themselves, do not blame yourself for what happened. There is nothing wrong with you. He just could not identify the diamond inside of you. You will heal from this, and one day you will marry the man who will love and value you. But you have to let him go. No matter if you believe he loves you or not, he made the choice to marry another person. Not you. I know it hurts to hear this, but you have to tell the truth to your heart, so that your heart can heal. As women, we have to learn to stop looking at a man's potential and face the hard-fact reality about him. He was inconsistent within your relationship, and he was unfaithful. Do what you need to do – cry, scream, talk about it until you get it ALL out of your system and then move on.

God saved you from what you couldn't save yourself from. You may not see it now, but one day you will hear how miserable he is in his life. The woman that he married may or may not be happy with him, but it's not your business. He is her problem now. But one thing that I can assure you is that he will never find another you. Let Go! Forgive him and move on. I wish you the best, and I know that one day things will turn around for your good.

Sincerely, Gurlé

"A man will feed his ego, before he feeds his heart."

-Caprice Lamor -

Letter-9

Dear Gurlé,

I grew up a *Church Girl.* Every Sunday without fail I had to attend church service. I was in the children's and adult's choir and on the Usher Board. I attended bible study and Sunday school services, and I also had to do volunteer work with the church. My entire life was church. My father is a pastor, and my mother is an evangelist. I couldn't wear nail polish, earrings, go to the movies with friends or be involved with school activities such as parties, sports or cheerleading. My parents were very strict. As far as boys go, FORGET IT. I couldn't have boys as friends. I wasn't allowed to go to my senior prom. I cried for days when that happened. My childhood wasn't horrible. I just feel that I missed out on a lot as a teenager. Today, I am thirty-one, and I still feel the pressure from my parents to be and live this righteous life. I could never make my own personal decisions about my life, because my parents are trying to relive their lives through me. After I graduated high school, I went to a college that my father wanted me to attend. I hated the school, but I did excellent academically, and I obtained a full scholarship. I also graduated one year early and continued onto my master's degree. My mother is a very submissive woman. She does whatever my father wants her to do, and she never questions his decisions. My mother never had a real job, and my father has always been the sole provider and disciplinarian of our home. I have one older brother. He wants to be exactly like my father. He works in the ministry at my father's church, and he is a "daddy pleaser." My brother lives for our father's approval. I recall a time when our first cousin received honors in his school. My father boasted about our cousin for weeks. My brother worked harder and the following semester received higher honors than our cousin. My brother excelled all through high school and college just to please our father. Everyone around me expects me to be perfect because I grew up a "PK" – that means Pastor's Kid. But the truth is I am not perfect. I am currently dating a guy whom most would call a "thug." He's been arrested in the past for distributing drugs (*He's always insisted that he never sold*

39

drugs in his life. He also insists that it was the people he was around that sold the drugs). My parents have no idea that I am in a relationship with him. I have my own home, which I worked very hard to get on my own (*without my parents' help*), and my boyfriend recently moved in with me. Whenever my mother stops by to pay me a visit, I have him leave the house for a few hours, so she doesn't suspect anything. My boyfriend knows about my parents and brother. He told me that church people are the first to judge him because of his past. This is why he doesn't attend church. He feels that "church folks" are the biggest hypocrites. However, I am still a very active member in my father's church. I sing every Sunday during both services and during Wednesday night bible study. I am "the voice" of our church. I've been told that God blessed me with the *gift of song*. But I feel like I am living a double life. Church people already are judged and criticized enough by the world. I don't want to be a hypocrite. I love God and I am a believer. I know that He is real. I'm just living with a man who is not my husband. Yes, we are engaging in sex, and yes, I am in love with him. I know that he is not the type of guy anyone I know would expect me to be with. But he is a smart guy, and he is a genius with math numbers. He even talks about going to school. He told me that I help him see life differently. Fast forward. Lately, I haven't been feeling too well at all. I went to the doctor assuming it was a head cold. They took some of my blood and gave me a pregnancy test, which I felt was a waste of time because I'm on the pill. But to my surprise, the test came back positive. I am pregnant. I am happy and scared all at the same time. I am doing very well in my career. I am a new homeowner. And I am also a "Church Girl" who happens to be pregnant by a man with an extensive jail record. I failed to mention that he also has two other children by two different women. He believes there is a God, but he doesn't believe in attending church. He strongly believes that all pastors do is take people's money, then give people a false hope that a man will appear from out of the clouds one day and save the world. My parents have no clue about my secret life with him. I met him before he went to jail one year ago. He had to complete a six-month sentence and when he was released, he blew my heart away and we made it official. We have secretly been together for over a year. Oh, how my family is going to enjoy this tea about me, because they've always been envious of my parents' financial lifestyle. My father's church is also going to have a gossip session about this. I don't know what to do. I don't want to be an embarrassment to my family. But I love this man, and I know that he is not the person people will think he is. He takes excellent care of his children, and he doesn't involve me in his relationship with his children's mother. He admitted that he was young and foolish when he got two girls pregnant at the same time. He was nineteen years old when it happened. I feel that if my father sat down and spoke with him, he would see that he is a young man who just started off on the wrong foot. He just needs some direction. I am having my baby. We love each other. We are talking about getting married and doing things the right way with this child. How do I tell my parents? I'm afraid that my father may never talk to me again. I will have to go before the church and repent for what I did and take responsibility for my actions. I know that God already has forgiven me. But it is true that "church folks" can be very judgmental. Please give me advice on how to approach this.

Sincerely, Church Girl

Dear Church Girl,

Hello and thank you for sharing your story. I can totally relate to what you are experiencing. I grew up in a Catholic church and my father was very stern. I know this is a hard situation, but you have to sit your parents down and tell them the truth. If your parents are truly representatives of God, they will be forgiving to you, and they will be there to give you wise counsel. Everyone is human, and we all make mistakes. Even though there are people in the world who feel that they have the right to judge you, God is the only one that can judge. You are a thirty-one-year-old young woman. You are financially providing for yourself, and you have fulfilled all the requirements the world tells us we need in order to become successful in life, such as having a college education and obtaining other degrees. You have to stop hiding behind your bible and be honest about who and where you are in your life. You have to stop pretending to live a life of perfection in the eyes of your parents, family and church family. The world will always talk about you no matter how good or bad you're doing. You cannot live your life for others, or you will never be happy. When you were younger, you had to abide by your parents' rules in their home. But you have your own home now, and no one can tell you how to live under your roof. The only person you have to answer to is God. I do understand your concern for the church and your father's reputation. No pastors want to learn that their children have become the same message they have preached against during a Sunday morning sermon. Every parent wants the best for their children. But you cannot concern yourself with opinions or gossip. God will deal with them, too. We all are sinners, and that is a known fact. If you love this young man and you believe that he is a good guy, go with your heart. But one thing I do know, you have to grow up and stop hiding from your parents like you're still a little girl. If you want their respect, you have to get respect for yourself. Contact your parents and tell them that you need to speak with them. Be bold, be strong and stick to your heart. Please contact me back to let me know how things worked out for you. You can do this. Just take a deep breath and pray before you meet with your parents. I promise you that everything will work out for you. Best wishes!

Sincerely, Gurlé

Dear Gurlé,

I wrote you three weeks ago about my life growing up as a *Church Girl.* I did what you recommended me to do. I called my father, and I asked if I could meet with him and my mother at the church after Sunday service and he agreed. I told my boyfriend that I've decided to tell my parents the truth about him. My boyfriend told me that he didn't want to cause any issues between me and my parents. He told me that he loves me and that he's willing to do whatever he needs to do to prove that he is a changed man. I met with my parents after church service. I waited until all the church members left the premises before conducting the meeting. I told my parents everything about my boyfriend, and my mother nearly passed out. My father just sat very quietly, and he listened very well. When I revealed that I was four months pregnant, I could see the tears fall from my father's eyes. My mother appeared to look excited, but she tried to hide it so no one would notice. After I told them everything, my father walked out of the room. My mother and I just sat quietly not knowing what would happen next. My father came back into the room a half hour later, and he apologized to me. I was confused. He told me that he was sorry that he failed me as a father. Of course, I started crying and then my mother was crying. He admitted that he sheltered me all my life and that he never allowed me to enjoy being a child, a teenager or even a young adult. He told me that he was a "Pastor's Kid." And that his father used to hit him with a wooden stick on his hand whenever he didn't get anything right the first time. My father told me perhaps if he'd allowed me to do the things that most teenagers did, I would have never hidden my life behind his back as an adult. My father told me that he wasn't angry with me and he'd done his part as my father by teaching me the word of God. He told me that I had to live my own life for me, not for him. He told me not to worry about the church. He would handle the situation in the appropriate manner. We all agreed that I would step down from the choir because I was beginning to show, and it was best for now. I was open and honest about my boyfriend's law issues. I told my father that I loved him and that he was a good guy. My parents were not too thrilled over the fact that he had two other children. But my father told me that he wanted to meet him. We arranged the meeting and the following night my parents met my boyfriend. My mother was very pleasant to him, but my father was very stern. He and my father left the room for three hours to talk privately in my father's home office. I was so nervous. I didn't know what to expect. My mother told me that she always hoped that I would marry before having children, and then she told me a little secret. She whispered to me that my brother was conceived before she and my father were married. She told me that my brother was born four months after her and my father were married. I was very surprised to hear that. After three long hours, my father and boyfriend came out of his office. Everything appeared to be good. We had dinner and we left to go home. It felt so good knowing that everything was finally out and in the open. My father addressed the church regarding me the Sunday that I did not attend church service. He told them very little details about me, and he only shared what they needed to know. There are some church members who are still whispering about me, and there are others who are genuinely happy for me. My boyfriend started attending church with me every Sunday. After attending our church for three months, my boyfriend joined and became a member. He is developing a strong relationship with God at his pace. He also will be attending community college in September, and our baby boy is due next year in January. One more thing I forgot to mention, we are engaged to be married. My father gave him his blessings. I don't know, but since that three-hour private meeting they had together, he and my father have become very close. I couldn't be happier. My fiancé also took a DNA test for his two daughters because both of his children's mothers were demanding more child support after learning he was engaged to me. I am happy that they did demand more money because the DNA tests revealed that he is not the father of either child. He also had to appear in court for another pending charge from two years ago and everything was dismissed. All his records were expunged. I am so grateful to God for everything! This is why we should never judge a book by its cover. What looked like a mess to the rest was a blessing in disguise from God for me. Thank you so much for your advice and words of encouragement.

Sincerely, Church Girl

Dear Church Girl,

I am so happy to hear that everything worked out well for you. It is very important in life that we don't judge other people because no one is perfect. You saw something in your "now" fiancé. You saw the goodness inside of him. But what really touched my heart is that your father recognized that although he is a pastor, he didn't do his best as your father by sheltering you. Sometimes parents can shelter their children so much that they cause more harm than good. Parents must allow their children to grow into who they are, while directing them with the right morals and values. If you teach a child the way they are supposed to go and they lose focus, they will find their way again. I am happy for your happy ending. It's not too often that stories such as yours end this way. Your parents did an excellent job raising you. You went with your heart. You never judged your fiancé's situation, and you accepted him for what you knew to be true in him and not by other people's opinions of him. Congratulations on your new life, new baby and your upcoming nuptials. You worked hard to become this woman right here, and you finally earned your parents' respect! Best wishes on everything.

Sincerely, Gurlé

You are beginning to break free...but not quite yet.

Dear Gurlé,

I've secretly been dealing with *Sexual Abuse* for years. When I was eight years old, my mother left me alone at home when she had to work. There was no one else to care for me. My mother was a single parent. I was the only child at that time. My mother later got into a relationship with a man, and she became pregnant with my sister two years later. My sister was born one week after my tenth birthday, and my mother's boyfriend moved in with us right after my sister's birth. My mother's boyfriend was very nice to me, and he truly appeared to love my mother. Shortly after my mother gave birth to my sister, she had to return to work. My mother worked in the medical field. She began working a new job at the hospital with better hours and pay. My mother's boyfriend worked as a garbage truck driver, but he had every weekend off. My mother made the decision to leave me and my baby sister with him when she worked nights and early morning shifts during the weekends. My mother trusted her boyfriend, and I felt comfortable being around him. It was fun in the beginning when my mother had to work. My mother's boyfriend always made me my favorite foods, and he would order us pizza at night. I looked forward to those weekends my mother had to work because my mother would never allow me to eat pizza every weekend or allow me to stay up late, camping out on the living room floor, watching movies. My mother's work hours increased as time went by, and she eventually received a job promotion. Things were going great. My mother was happy and in love with my sisters' father. They often spoke about marriage. I was excited, too. I really liked my mother's boyfriend, and I wanted them to get married so he could become my father. As the year went by, my body started to change. I began developing breasts. My mother was a very shapely lady. I was often told as I matured that I looked like a younger version of my mother.

49

On my eleventh birthday, I began my menstrual cycle, and my body just developed more overnight. One day, my life changed in the blink of an eye. My mother was working as usual. I was in the shower, and my mother's boyfriend walked in while I was completely naked. I felt so embarrassed. He immediately apologized to me. He told me he didn't know that I was in the bathroom. As he just stood there staring at me, he told me that I was developing into a beautiful young lady. I just stood there as I held the towel over my cold, naked body. I didn't know what to say. I felt awkward. He left the bathroom, and I quickly got dressed. When I came out of the bathroom, he assured me that there was nothing for me to be embarrassed about. He insisted that he didn't mean to walk in on me, and he asked me to keep what happened between just us two. I felt better. I thought nothing more about it. The next day, my mother had to leave for work much earlier than usual. She was scheduled to work until the next morning. Later that night, I was in the living watching television, and my mother's boyfriend walked into the room. He sat on the living room sofa behind me as I continued to lie on the floor. He asked me if I had a boyfriend, and I told him no, I was too young to have a boyfriend. He told me if I ever had any questions about boys that I could always talk to him about it. As I continued to watch television, he sat on the floor next to me. The next thing I felt is his hand underneath the cover. He began fondling my private area with his fingers. I didn't know what to do. I was frozen. I didn't tell him to stop, and I didn't push him away. He pulled down my pajamas and he performed oral sex on me. I didn't understand what was happening. He whispered in my ear to relax and he penetrated me. After he was finished, he got up as if nothing happened. In the days to come, he started buying me gifts and giving me money. My mother didn't notice a thing because she was in love with him. One day, when he learned that I had a boyfriend he became very upset. He walked into my room, and he questioned me about my relationship with my boyfriend. He told me to break up with him. My mother overheard him talking to me in my room, and she asked him what was going on. He told my mother that he was not going to take care of any children if I became pregnant. My mother told him that he was not my father, and that she was not worried about me getting pregnant. He and my mother argued about me the entire night. He told my mother that he had been a father figure to me and that he didn't appreciate her telling him what he could say to me. My mother told me to not tell him anything about my boyfriend ever again. That same night, he threatened to leave my mother. He told her that he wasn't happy with her anymore. My mother cried and begged him not to leave her. She told him that she would do anything for him. I couldn't believe that all of that was happening because I had a boyfriend. My mother was so blind. I couldn't believe that she didn't see the signs. She was always weak when it came down to men. During the days my mother was working, her boyfriend continued having sex with me. I started to like it, and I began to like him, too. There were times I tried to tell myself that it wasn't normal. But he made me feel so special and important. He made me promise to break up with my boyfriend and I did. I didn't want him and mother to be together anymore. Because I loved him. At least I thought I did. Today, I am nineteen, and I don't trust him with my little sister. She is about to be the age that I was when he started sexually abusing me. My sister looks like my mother, too. She's becoming well developed in her body. I still engage in sex with him, but not as often as we use to. I've never told anyone about what happened. But today, I FINALLY understand what he did to me was wrong. I feel ashamed and disgusted. I feel that he is after my sister, too. I could tell by the way that he looks at her and the way that he treats her. He did the same things to me. If I tell my mother now, she may hate me or think that I am lying. I'm afraid. Everything is my fault because I didn't say no, I didn't tell him to stop. I agreed

51

by engaging in sex with him all of these years until now. I don't know what to do. I don't want to break my mother's heart. I feel strongly in my heart that he has already got to my sister. What should I do? Please help me.

Sincerely, Sexual Abuse

Dear Sexual Abuse,

Thank you for being such a brave young lady. There are many girls and women in this world right now who were sexually abused or are currently being sexually abused today. The first thing I need you to know is THIS WAS NOT YOUR FAULT! You were a child, and your mother trusted that person to care for you in her absence. You did NOTHING wrong. You didn't understand what was happening to you. What your mother's boyfriend did to you all of these years was wrong. Someone needs to know what happened to you. If you don't feel secure that you will get support from your mother, it's important that you share what happened to you with someone, especially if you strongly believe that he is sexually abusing your sister right now. There could be other young girls that he has done this to. Is there anyone that you can call that you trust? Have you shared this with anyone else? I know that this is all overwhelming for you. Although I told you this was not your fault, I know that you blame yourself because you liked it and felt that you loved him, too. But please understand that you were a child. He manipulated you, and you were confused. You couldn't identify right from wrong because an adult that you trusted made you feel like what he was doing was okay. But it was wrong. You are not the only girl that this has ever happened to. There are young girls all around the world who were made to feel special by family members, friends and strangers who were sexually inappropriate with them. They tell you not to share what happened and to keep it a secret. They also make you believe if you tell someone, they would blame you for the family or marriages falling apart. But it's all a lie. They tell you these things because they know they are wrong, and if you, and the other sexual abuse victims, tell someone what they did to you, they would go to jail. I need you to share what you told me to someone immediately, and then report this information to your local police department. Do not be concerned about your mother's feelings or if you will get your mother's support. You are nineteen years old. You have a voice to speak out for yourself. You will get the support that you need, even if it's not from your family. You will get the support. I need you to understand that once you share what happened to you, a lot of things are going to happen. But whatever you do, tell your story, and tell the truth. I don't want you to be upset if he lies and says that it never happened and that you've always had a crush on him. He may say a lot of things about you that are untrue to discredit your accusations against him. But you stick to your truth no matter what. Your mother may or may not believe you, but you stick to your truth. Your sister may never admit that he sexually abused her, and she may be convinced by your mother or her father to say that you are a liar. But no matter what the outcome is, you stick to your truth. Don't ever change your truth for anyone's lies. You are a strong, courageous young lady, and I applaud you for your bravery. There are grown women today who are not brave enough to do what you are about to do. Below I provided you with a number for the Child Abuse Hotline. Call them; they can also help guide you. Please keep me informed about what happens. I will be waiting to hear back from you. REMEMBER, THIS WAS NOT YOUR FAULT, AND YOU DID NOTHING WRONG. Adults are supposed to protect children when in their care, not hurt, abuse or harm them. Thank you for reaching out. I'm expecting to hear back from you.

Sincerely, Gurlé

Childhelp National Child Abuse Hotline: If you suspect that a child has been harmed or is at risk of being harmed by abuse or neglect, call 1-800-4-A-CHILD (1-800-422-4453). If you believe a child is in immediate danger of harm, call 911 first.

Child Welfare Information Gateway: Visit this site for information on state-level government resources for reporting abuse or neglect, www.childwelfare.gov.

Dear Gurlé,

I reached out to you some months ago regarding the *Sexual Abuse* that I've experienced by my mom's boyfriend since the age of eleven. I wanted to update you on everything that transpired since we last wrote each other. After I reached out to you, you suggested that I confide in someone I trust. I decided to disclose everything that happened to me to my best friend's mom. I told her every intricate detail from age eleven until now. The first thing that she stated to me is that I did nothing wrong. It was a relief to finally get it all out to someone that I could trust. She asked me if my mom ever noticed any signs of the abuse, and I told her no. She told me that it was best for me to report what happened to our local police department. She told me that she would go with me and she would be by my side the entire way. That evening we went to the police department, and I told my truth as you told me to do. I expressed to the authorities my concerns for my nine-year-old sister. I told them that I believed he is abusing her as well. After they took my statement, Child Protective Services was contacted, and they sent a social worker to the home to speak with my mom and sister. They also sent a police officer to the home to speak with my mom's boyfriend. It was all happening so fast. My heart was pounding. I was fearful of what my mom's response would be. My sister admitted to the social worker during the interview with her that sexual abuse did occur with her father. She told the social worker that it first happened three months ago, at night, while everyone was sleeping. Her father performed oral sex on her, and he made her perform oral sex on him, too, just before he sexually penetrated her. She told the social worker the second time it happened was also at night while everyone was sleeping. My mom's boyfriend was arrested and charged with sexual abuse against a minor. My mom was so angry at me and my sister. She told the social worker that she knew that he would never do anything to hurt his daughter. She also told the social worker that I was very promiscuous and that I had a boyfriend. She told the social worker that she always knew that I had a crush on her man because of the way I used to act around him. I knew at that moment I could no longer stay at my mom's house after that happened. I was hurt that my own mom didn't believe me. She had the audacity to tell her boyfriend that she was following them to the police station. She was going to bail him out of jail. My younger sister was crying hysterically. I told her that it was okay, and that I will support her through all of this. My best friend's mom told me that I was welcome to come and stay with her as long as I needed. I knew that my relationship with my mom would never be the same again. My mom blamed me for coaching my sister to say these things about her father. My mom was advised by Child Protective Services that her boyfriend was not allowed to stay in the home with my sister even if she bailed him out of jail. My mom really lost her mind. She told the social worker to take my sister if they felt that she was in danger. She went on and on about how she worked hard all of her life to care and provide for my sister and me. And this is the "Thank You" that she gets from us. My mom behaved this way and said all these things in front of the social worker, and they temporarily removed my sister from my mom's care. My best friend's mom agreed to take my sister with her so my sister would not be placed in a foster home. The next day, my mom paid bail to have him released from jail. My sister later recanted her story and said that she made it all up. But because I was a minor when her father sexually abused me, he was still being charged by the prosecutor's office. One month later, my sister went back home with my mom after her father agreed to leave the home until the case was completely investigated by Child Protective Services. I don't know what my mom did or said to my sister, but she continued to deny all the accusations. My sister's father also denied that he ever touched me. He told the police that I walked around the house dressed inappropriately showing parts of my body. He stated that I was always trying to get his attention, but he knew better. My sister never did change her story back, and she continued to deny that any sexual abuse ever occurred. The case with Child Protective Services was closed months later, and my sister's father moved back into the house with my mom. My mom disowned me. She called me names that I would never call my worst enemy. My mom accused me of being "jealous" of her and wanting "her man." Since then, I have not spoken with my mom, nor seen her boyfriend. Tomorrow is my twentieth birthday. I still live with my best friend's mom, and I am attending community college. I have a job, and I recently purchased a used car for myself. I'm just taking one day at a time. My sister discreetly called me two weeks ago. She disclosed to me that her father is still sexually abusing her, and he hurt her one night. She could barely walk the next day. My sister told me that she believes our mom knows what he is doing to her, but she just doesn't want to accept it. She told me that our mom treats her badly, and she doesn't want to be there with her anymore. I called Child Protective Services anonymously to report my concerns, but my mom knew when they showed back up to the home that it was me who called. She left a very nasty message on my phone, and she even threatened to fight me in the streets. Since then, I have not heard from my sister. The cell phone number my sister had is disconnected. I don't know what happened when Child Protective Services went back to the home to investigate. I don't know if my sister denied the accusations again. I just hope that one day my sister will finally tell her TRUTH to someone as I have told my TRUTH. I don't know how else to help my sister, and I feel horrible about it. As of today, the charges are currently pending against my mom's boyfriend for what he did to me as a minor. He is currently facing three to five years in prison. I recently learned that he proposed to my mom, and they went to the courthouse and got married. My mom is also pregnant with another baby girl by him. Thank you for all your help and guidance. I would have never had the courage to tell someone if it were not for you. I will always tell my TRUTH in my life as you have encouraged me to do no matter what!

Sincerely, Sexual Abuse

Dear Sexual Abuse,

Thank you for responding back to me. Wow is what I really want to say, but instead I will say this to you, "YOU DID NOTHING WRONG!" I am so proud of you and your courage to do what you did. I know that it hurts, that you didn't get the support that you needed from your mother. But you got the support from your best friend's mother, and you weren't alone. You did all you could to help your sister. There is not much you could do for her until she is old enough to speak out without your mother's interference. Just continue to be there for her when she calls you and listen to her. If you feel you need to keep reporting what she shares with you to Child Protective Services, keep reporting. Eventually, she will tell her truth, too. I am happy to hear that you are in school. Keep moving forward and stay positive. You've been through so much in your life. I want to recommend that you speak with a counselor or a therapist about the abuse and your relationship with your mother. It will help you begin the healing process as you grow older. No matter if your mother decides to never speak to you again, you have to keep telling yourself that YOU DID NOTHING WRONG. Your mother will have to face her choices one day and all the things she did wrong in this matter. You may or may not receive an apology from your mother, and your sister may never tell her truth. But whatever happens, you must continue living and being the best you that you can be, despite all that has happened to you. One day, you will have to forgive your mother and her boyfriend FOR YOU. You may not feel forgiveness in your heart today. But eventually, your heart WILL heal, and you will be able to forgive them. I also know that it's going to be hard for you to trust people, especially men. But do know that not all men in this world are like your mother's boyfriend. One day, you will find the right love, and he will love you the way you are supposed to be loved. And I promise you it won't hurt. Thank you again for sharing and being brave. You just helped save a lot of females with your story.

Sincerely, Gurlé

58

"Stand in your
TRUTH even when
they stand in their
lies."
- Caprice Lamor -

Dear Gurlé,

I am a *Mixed Girl.* My father and mother are two completely different races. All of my life I have been asked this one question: "*What are you?*" – the one question that I've always tried to avoid because it's sort of rude. I went through this in school and even now as an adult, it seems to be worse. If I acknowledge part of my race and not the other, I'm told that I am ashamed of my other race. If I recognize them both equally, I'm told that I have to choose which race I identify with the most. It's a sad world to live in when they make a person feel badly about their own identity. I just want to be me, not my mother's race or my father's race, just me. I am a nice person, and I have the funniest humor. If only people could say hello and ask me my name before wanting to know "what I am" or "where I come from" as if I come from another planet. I am a Mixed Girl. I get it, my hair looks different, my complexion is awkward and my eyes are rare. But I am still a human being. My closest friends have teased me about it, and they have referred to me as a "mutt," like a mixed dog. I used to laugh with them when they called me that in the past, but truthfully, their comments have always hurt my feelings. I don't want to choose one part of me over the other. Therefore, I don't want anyone else to choose which side of my race to affiliate or identify me with. I want all of who I am to be acknowledged. And I refuse to allow anyone to choose or pick a side of me. I am also tired of explaining every day to individuals that my mom is from here, and my dad is from there. How about this, I came from out of my mother's womb after she carried me for nine months. That's what I really want to tell them. What upsets me the most is that I've developed identity issues, as well as low self-esteem, due to this. I'm not as outgoing as I use to be. I don't care to meet new people anymore, and I have always been a people person. I love meeting people from all over the world. I now find that

I hide myself a lot, and I am ashamed of who I am. I've never been this person in my life. I have always been confident in who I was, but lately I hide. I don't want to become this person that society is trying to force me to become. I don't want to have to explain my identity every day to people, nor be judged because of my identity. I'd rather a person judge me by my character than by my appearance, my culture, my race, or my religion. If the world could see people for their hearts, this world will be a better place to live. I'm trying to find me again, the Mixed Girl who once was okay with being a Mixed Girl. How can I get back to her? How do I learn to love and accept everything about her again without allowing other people's judgement to interfere? Please help?

Sincerely, Mixed Girl

Dear Mixed Girl,

Thank you for reaching out to me. I just want to say to you that you never lost yourself. You never lost who you were. You just allowed the world to make you doubt who you KNEW you've always been. It happens to the best of us. You carried the world's views and opinions of you when you should have never picked them up from the beginning. Just be who you are, and don't allow anyone to force you to make that choice. The next person that asks you, *"What are you?"* nicely respond with, *"I'm a person."* You don't have to keep explaining your genetics to anyone. If you choose to share your background history with others, then it's okay. And if you don't choose to share, then that's okay, too. It doesn't sound to me like you have low self-esteem or identity issues. It appears the only identity issues that you've experienced came from not being able to "identify" with what others think of this world. Keep being who you once were before. Get back out there and be the friendly Mixed Girl that you are and walk with your head held high. You do know that it is okay to tell people you're not comfortable with discussing certain topics about yourself, such as your identity. People will respect your feelings, and if not, then make them respect you. You don't owe any further explanations to anyone about you or your ethnicity. If you train yourself to close your ears to the negative vibrations of this world, you will only leave the sounds of the positive and beautiful melodies that are often unheard. Just be you, love you and accept you even if the world finds a hard time accepting the many diversities of you. Eventually, they will catch up. Well, most of them will. The other percentage is not your concern. Be great, but again BE YOU! I wish you the best!!

Sincerely, Gurlé

Dear Gurlé,

I'm *Gay*. I've always known that I was, but I pretended to like boys because I was afraid. Being Gay is still not as accepted by people in the world today. If you look at my family background, you'd never suspect that I would be this way. I grew up in a strict household. Both of my parents were very stern. My parents are happily married today. I have one sister and one brother. I am the youngest child. I just turned twenty-six two weeks ago. I cannot believe that I am finally sharing this secret with someone. I've held it in for so long. The guys in my school always liked me. I have what they consider is a nice body, which I've always hated. I did anything to cover up my breasts and my body. I've always worn oversized clothing, but in school, during gym class, I couldn't hide too much because of the uniform. The boys in school used to go crazy over my body. I felt disgusted deep down inside whenever a boy flirted with me, but because I am a girl, I pretended to be flattered by their comments. When I was fifteen, I had my first experience with a girl. I fell in love with a girl from my high school. She was pretty. I've always felt that she liked me, too. I can't explain it, but it was a secret code that we spoke to each other without uttering one word. A code that we wouldn't even break to each other. I guess we both were protecting our secret identity. We became like best friends, and we started having sleepovers at each other's homes. I've always excelled academically in school. I was in all honor classes and she was, too. Our parents weren't friends, but they allowed us to hang out and to have sleepovers at each other houses, because they knew we were best friends. My parents also trusted her parents because of their family background. During one sleepover at her house one night, we shared a kiss and made out. She told me that she always liked girls, but she could never share it with anyone because she was too afraid. We were each others' first experience. I liked what we did that night. She made me feel good. I didn't know what was happening to me, but I began to feel confused. We both were females, and I knew that girls are supposed to like boys in that way, not a girl. It was easy for me and her to be together because we were girls, and no one ever suspected anything. During my senior year in high school, I met another girl two years older than me. She really turned me out in ways that I never thought, and I fell in love with her. I broke my girlfriend's heart when I broke up with her. I imagined it hurt her like a guy breaking up with a girl. She went crazy, and she started cutting herself, but her family never knew why. I lost contact with her since I graduated high school and went onto college and graduated. Today, I am in a new, but secret, relationship with a girl who looks more like a boy. My parents and friends are beginning to ask me questions about my relationship status. My mother is pressuring me to meet a guy, so I can get married and have a family, but I believe that my father knows I'm a lesbian. He tried to spark up the conversation with me one day, but I dodged the conversation, and he never tried again. I come from a family that is highly respected in our community. Both my parents have made a financial and educational impact in our community. Both of my siblings are married with children. Yet, I have never brought a guy home once, not even to my high school senior prom. I went to my prom alone. The truth is that I'm in love with my current girlfriend. She makes me feel good and secure about who I am. I am tired of hiding who I am to my family and friends. I don't want to be judged, but I can't help who I love. I can't help what I feel inside. I tried to like boys, but it always felt weird and very uncomfortable for me. I know people who came out to their family and they were disowned by them. Now they are homeless and living in the street. I don't want my family to disown me. But I know this is going to break my mother's heart. I am her youngest child. But I have to be true to who I am. I can no longer hide this secret. I am Gay, and I love women. Wow, it felt good to say that. Now I just need to find the heart to tell my

65

parents. What if my parents disown me? What if I lose my female friends who never knew I liked girls? They may think that I liked them, too. Just because a woman is Gay, it doesn't mean that she likes all women, just like men don't like every girl. I do have my preferences. I don't want to be looked at weird. I definitely don't want to make anyone feel uncomfortable, but I have to free myself from this secret life that I've been living since I was fifteen years old. My girlfriend is also tired of me hiding her, too. Her family knows that she's a lesbian. They are not happy about it, but they have learned to accept it. Do you think I should tell my family or continue living this secret life? My entire world is going to change once I tell the people I love the most. There are a few people who I know suspects that I am Gay, and my father is one of them. I guess I am scared. I've heard the saying, "*God made Adam and Eve, not Adam and Steve.*" But God also is love, right? Am I wrong for loving someone who looks like me? Why can't we love who we love and it be okay? I just want to be honest about who I am without being judged by the world and the people who I love the most. Please help.

Sincerely, Gay

Dear Gay,

I want to thank you for being bold and for allowing me to be the first person you openly come out to. This is very brave of you. It must have been difficult pretending to be something that you weren't for all those years. I know you may have questioned at times if what you were going through was just a phase or who you truly were. I just want to start off by saying, I would never judge you. However, people are entitled to have their personal opinions and beliefs about what they feel. For many people, it would be good to live in a world where people could love who they choose to love, no matter their gender. Unfortunately, that is not the reality of the world we live in. But despite the world's views and opinions, you have to live your best life for you, even if your parents don't accept nor agree with your lifestyle or preferences. You still have to live your life for you. No one can control your heart. People cannot force a person's heart to unlove the things their heart loves. You should be honest with yourself first before you are honest with anyone else. If this is who you believe you are, then be truthful to that person. Let today be the last day that you live in a lie. I'm going to be very transparent with you. You may lose some friendships, and family members may turn their backs on you. You may be told that this is not of God and that it is a sin to be with the same sex. You may be made to feel sinful and dirty. But whatever happens, know that God loves you no matter who you love, no matter how you look, no matter your skin color, no matter the sins that you may or may not commit. God loves you. He knows everything, and he sees and knows your heart. God understands us more than we understand ourselves. If your parents decide to turn their back on you, give them some time to process everything. In due time, your parents will come around, and they will embrace you because you are their child. And if they never come around after all, you have to remain truthful to you. Please keep me posted on what happens. Let me know

67

what transpired after you disclosed your truth to your family and friends. Always remember, be true to you first. Below is a hotline number for you or any person that is in need of Gay, Bisexual, Transgender or Lesbian support. Please share with anyone that you feel may need it. I wish you the best!!

Sincerely, Gurle

<u>LGBT National Hotline</u>: The LGBT hotline provides support to those in need via the following times 1-888-843-4564, Monday-Friday, 4pm -12am and Saturday noon– 5pm, EST. You can also reach this hotline through e-mail at help@LGBThotline.org.

Dear Gurlé,

I wrote you a letter two months ago disclosing to you that I am *Gay*. I want to thank you for your encouraging words. They really gave me the confidence that I needed to come out to my family and friends. I came out to my parents three weeks after I received your letter. My father suspected that I was Gay. He told me that he always knew deep down inside. He told me that he loved me no matter what and that I would always be his baby girl. My mother on the other hand, she has yet to accept that I am Gay. She is convinced that this is a phase that I am going through and that it will go away soon. She has been trying to connect me with her friend's son who is my age, and she has been purposely having functions so I could meet a guy. My mother refuses to meet my girlfriend, but my father met her over dinner two nights ago. As far as my siblings, they don't care. My siblings treat me the same way. They are looking forward to meeting my girlfriend. My friends also said that they knew that I was Gay, too. They were all just waiting for me to finally come out. Meanwhile, my mother has been quoting more scriptures to me and telling me how God is not pleased, and that women were created to be with a man. My mother is also devastated that I may never have children. My mother also invited me to her church and had her priest pray for me. I was so embarrassed. The entire church knows that I'm a lesbian because of my mother. I should have known she was up to something when she invited me. My mother said to me the other day that I am such a pretty girl and that I am wasting my time by being in a relationship with another woman. She had the audacity to ask me how we have sex. She asked me if we lay on top of each other or pushed objects inside each other's vaginas for pleasure. I must admit, I had to laugh when she asked me that. I couldn't believe what I was hearing. My mother and I also had words once, when she overheard me on the phone telling my girlfriend goodnight and that I loved her. My mother told me that we were living in sin and that we were going to hell. I recognize that it's going to take my mother some time to get adjusted to the fact that her daughter is a Gay woman. This is not a phase; this is who I am. Remember the girl that I had my first experience with when I was fifteen years old? I ran into a mutual friend of ours prior to me writing you the first letter. They told me that she committed suicide last year. She finally came out to her family after all of these years, and her family disowned her. Her father took her being Gay the hardest. She had a very close relationship with him; she was a "daddy's girl." When her father told her that he wanted nothing to do with her, she couldn't handle it. I felt so sad after hearing the news. I know I had nothing to do with her prior issues. They were deeper than I'll ever know. I just wanted to take this time to thank you again for just listening. I hope in time my mother grows to accept that I AM GAY.

Sincerely, Gay

Dear Gurlé,

I am a *Single Mother,* and I am raising a son on my own. My son's father and I ended our relationship when I was four months pregnant. My son's father pretended he was going to be involved in our son's life, but after our son was born, he had another child with another woman. It's been rough trying to raise my son on my own without his father's help. It hurts even more when I learned that his father is very involved with his other child's life. My son just turned nine years old, and he's beginning to ask me a lot of questions. Questions that I would never expect a nine-year-old to ask their parent. He is a very smart young man, and my son watches everything that I do and that scares me. I don't want my son to mimic any of my female behaviors that he sees me displaying. My son watches me as I get dressed and how I walk when I put on my heels. One day, I caught him trying to walk in my heels like me. I know that there is nothing wrong with my son's sexuality. But I don't have any men around my son, and he only sees me. Any guys that I have dated in the past, I never introduced them to my son. I promised myself if my relationships weren't leading to anything serious, they would never meet my son. Lately, my son's attitude has been bad in school, and he has been challenging my authority and being defiant towards me at home. I have to be honest with you. One day, he was playing with matches, and I slapped him in his face. I don't want to result to beating my child because I don't believe that is the only way to discipline your children. But I am having a hard time with him. I'm stressed and overwhelmed. I have been called to his school four times this month. They wanted to suspend him for starting a fight with another student. I called his father, and once again, he pretended that he was going to be there. He made arrangements two weeks ago to pick up our son, but he never showed up. My son sat at the window all day waiting for his father to come. My son called his father to see when he was coming to get him, and his father didn't answer his phone. There is no one that I can turn to for direction. My father was never in my life, and my mother died when I was five years old. I grew up in foster care my entire life. I am working and attending community college. I'm just trying to make a life for me and my son. I don't want to ask the school for help because they are quick to classify my son. My son does not have ADHD, and he doesn't need to be on medication. My hair is falling out, and my job is threatening to fire me because every time I turn around, I have to call out of work to meet with my son's teachers. I'm trying not to give up, but I'm tired. I don't know what else to do. I'm afraid that I'm going to physically hurt my son, and I don't want to cause him any harm. The school already contacted Child Services because he was caught playing with matches on the school premises. Thank God the case was closed out quickly. I just need some guidance on what to do. I don't have all the answers. I grew up in the system, so it's hard for me to trust anyone with my son. I just need some advice on what to do. I feel like I am at my last end.

Sincerely, Single Mother

Dear Single Mother,

Thank you for reaching out, but most importantly, thank you for admitting that you cannot do it all alone. Motherhood is one of the hardest and toughest roles on the planet. Motherhood doesn't come with instructions, and you never know what to expect as each day comes. Are there any right or wrong answers to being a parent? You just learn as you go. There is no such thing as a perfect parent. It doesn't matter if both parents are involved or not. It's a huge responsibility that not even life could prepare you for. I just want you to know what you're feeling is normal. Most mothers go through these same emotions and feelings, especially when raising a son. I understand that you grew up in foster care, and you are very protective of who you have around your son. But there is nothing wrong with seeking outside resources. There are mentorship and Big Brother programs, sports and other activities that your son can get involved with. I know that these resources could be beneficial and helpful for you. They will also get you the support that you need. It sounds like your son is going through the typical stages of growth. He needs to be more involved with other activities besides school, and he needs to be around positive males, so he can have someone to look up to. I admire that you are very cautious about who you bring around your son. That is important. However, it's also important that you expose your son to male figures, especially those who can help and be a support to you. I also agree that not all children who are acting out should immediately be classified with ADHD. Most children will test their parent's patience and even their schoolteacher's on purpose to see if they can get away with it. But it shouldn't be that all bad behavior means classifying a child with a learning or behavior disorder. I also recommend that you find someone you can talk to, perhaps another mother? Or someone that could relate to where you mentally are right now. In order to meet mothers like yourself, you need to show yourself friendly and slowly open up

73

to building trust and new friendships. Is there a sport that your son likes to play? Get him involved in sports. That will be a great way for him to learn discipline and to learn how to become a team player. You also need to build yourself a support team. I know that you're used to doing it all alone, but you don't have to. I'm sure there are support groups out there for single mothers. You don't have to feel stressed and overwhelmed when there are many resources out there for mothers like you. Below I will provide you with a list of resources for mentorship and Big Brother programs for your son, as well as support groups for you, too. Please keep me posted on your son's progression and remember that you are not alone. Thank you for reaching out, and I look forward to hearing back from you.

Sincerely, Gurlé

Big Brother Big Sisters Nationwide Program: The goal of this organization is to see children achieve success by connecting children with mentors. To learn more, contact www.bbbssepa.org.

Team Single Moms Planet: This site provides information ranging from financial literacy to family fun activities for single mothers. For more information, visit their site: Singlemomsplanet.com.

Dear Gurlé,

I wrote you three months ago about the struggles of being a *Single Mother.* I took your advice, and I signed my son up to play football. I found a local football team around our neighborhood. I met with the coach, and he told me to bring my son to the next game practice. My son did extremely well. I didn't know that he could run so fast. I also met two mothers; their sons have been playing on the same football team for the past two years. They were really nice to me. They helped me feel much better about the things I've been experiencing with my son. It turns out that they went through similar situations as well. They told me they help each other out by taking turns picking up and dropping the boys off to practice. I decided to join in the club. This arrangement has helped me a great deal. On top of that, my son is doing much better in school; he's making all A's. My son and I agreed that if he didn't make good grades, no football. And he loves football. His coach told me that my son has the potential to play professional football one day because of his speed. My son makes two touchdowns per game. He is the little star of his team. I am so proud! I am also happy to report that his father came to his last two games. There is no consistency with him, but I'm happy that he is making the effort. My son loves his coach, and he looks up to him. The coach spends time with my son and two other boys outside of football. He takes them fishing and to basketball games. I am so glad that I reached out to you. I would have never opened up to anyone in the past. I realize that it's okay to share a little about yourself without giving your entire life story. The phones are no longer ringing from my son's school and everything is good. I just want to thank you again for your advice and your help.

Sincerely, Single Mother

Dear Gurlé,

I'm twenty-eight, and I am a victim of *Domestic Violence.* I've never shared this with anyone, and I never thought that this would happen to me. I've seen and heard about other women being physically, verbally, and emotionally abused in their relationships. But I never thought that I would be that girl. I met my significant other when I was twenty-five. He is seven years older than me. One day, I was walking down the street and as he passed by me, he softly whispered *"Can I come."* In the midst of the busy loud traffic, I heard his voice. When I turned around, he began to walk towards me. He asked me for my name and number. But he didn't have a pen or paper to write down my number. He said that he had a good memory. I didn't believe him, but I gave him my number anyway. I thought nothing more about it. A few days later I received a call from him, and that's where it all began. He was very charming, tall and good looking. He made me feel like I was the most beautiful girl in the world. We dated for months before we became serious with each other. I thought that I had struck gold. He was everything that a girl would want in a guy. We were inseparable and we did everything together. After dating for a year, we moved in together, and things were going well. I started a new job, which required me to work late hours at times. He also had a good paying job, but he later was fired. He never disclosed to me why he was fired. I also wasn't too concerned, because I was able to handle all the bills with my salary alone. One evening, my girlfriend and I decided to have a girls night out. We hadn't hung out since I began my relationship with him. I was excited, and I desperately needed my girl time with my friend. I was getting dressed to leave when he walked into our bedroom. He asked me where I was going, and I told him out with my girlfriend. He told me that he didn't like my friend I was going out with because she receives a lot of male attention. He made it clear that he didn't want me being around her (*The only other friend I have he approves of has six children, and she is in a bad relationship with her children's father. But, for whatever reasons, he has no issues with me hanging out with her*). We got into such a heated discussion that I ended up cancelling my night out with my friend. As months went by, he began isolating me more from my friends and family. Every time I wanted to meet up with some girlfriends, or go visit with my family members, it always turned into a huge argument. And I always allowed him to win. One particular night, after we had a terrible disagreement, I left the house to meet up with one of my closest girlfriends. I honestly needed a mental break away from him. When I returned home later that night, nothing could have prepared me for what was to come. I unlocked the front door, and as I entered my apartment, I felt his fist against my face. It happened so quickly, I had no time to react. After he punched me several times on my face, he called me inappropriate names. He consistently called me a bitch. He told me that I wasn't shit to him, but a whore. He then accused me of cheating on him with another man. He also threatened to kill the man that I allegedly was cheating with once he found out who he was. I just laid on the floor holding my face as I cried. I was in excruciating pain. My lip was beginning to swell, and I could taste the blood inside of my mouth. He sat next to me on the floor and he screamed at me, "*Why did you make me hit you?*" He cried and he asked me to forgive him. He told me he was sorry and that he felt like complete shit. He said, "*I've never loved a woman the way that I love you.*" He begged me not to leave him. He laid next to me on the floor as he sobbed. I silently cried. He assured me that he would never hit me again and that he hit me out of fear of losing me. I was gullible. I believed him. We hugged and that night we made passionate love. As he made love to me, he told me that he was going to make me his wife. I was in love with him, and I forgave him because he had a terrible childhood growing up. He shared with me that in the past he was sexually and physically abused as a child. His parents were addicted to drugs,

77

and he was raised in a foster home. I thought that I could save him and give him the love that he always needed. As time moved forward, the verbal abuse worsened, and he became more controlling. He once showed up unexpectedly to my work place causing a scene. He accused every guy in my work place of liking me. We would argue outside of my job building, and he would call me a slut and a bitch. He assured me there were plenty of girls out there he could be with who were prettier than me. I am thankful that no one from my workplace ever saw us. I continued to take the abuse for months. One year had gone by, and I hadn't seen or spoken with my close friends or family. He made me change my cell phone and house numbers. He also forced me to give him my passwords to my email and phone, but he would never give me his passwords. He told me that was his personal business. I slowly began to lose myself. I no longer recognized myself. During the days at work, I pretended to be happy. But I was miserable and afraid. One day, I didn't want to have sex with him, but he forced me to. When he was done, he spit in my face, and he proceeded to call me ugly. He constantly reminded me that no other man would ever want me. I believed him. I no longer liked myself either. After the constant abuse from him, I finally got the strength to tell him that it was over and that I didn't want the relationship anymore. He took a knife from the kitchen draw and threatened to take his life. I pleaded with him to put the knife away because I didn't want him to harm himself. He told me he would put the knife away if I stayed. He begged me not to leave him. I promised him that I would stay, but deep down inside I desperately wanted out. After he tried to kill himself things were calm. He was treating me better. I thought to myself, *"Maybe our relationship will work after all."* So, I thought. But I was wrong. I remember this day very clearly because I saw this actress wearing a beautiful gown on television. I told him how much I admired her gown and in that moment he snapped at me. He told me he's always known that I was a whore. He then grabbed me by my neck, and he nearly choked the air out of my body. I managed to escape from him, and I ran out of my apartment door. I ran as far away as I could from my apartment building, and I called my friend *(the one that he likes)* to come and pick me up. She came within minutes, and she took me to the hospital. At the hospital, the nurse tried to get me to confess that I was hurt in a domestic dispute. But I told her I had accidentally tripped and fallen down some stairs. The nurse knew that I was not being truthful with her. My girlfriend tried to convince me he was a good guy and that he really loved me. That was why he hit me. I was later released from the hospital and prescribed pain medication. When I arrived back to my apartment, he cried again. He told me the same sob story, how he was sorry. He made another promise to never hit me again. Less than two hours later, he was cursing me out again. This time, he told me that he should have *"killed me."* I felt alone. I didn't know who I could turn to. He isolated me from all my friends and family. I still hadn't seen my mother in a year. I had no way of calling anyone when at work because he would take my cell phone with him to monitor my phone calls. I didn't know anyone's number by memory, and I couldn't write anyone's numbers on paper because he watched my every move at home. I had to think of a plan. I had to get out of this abusive relationship. But he always found a way to convince me that he was sorry and that he would never do it again. One night, I got off of work earlier than usual. My coworker, who is a happily married man, drove me home because my boyfriend had my vehicle. When he saw me getting out of my coworker's vehicle, he gave my coworker a fake smile. As my coworker waved goodbye and drove away, my boyfriend softly touched the back of my neck, as he murmured under his breath, *"I'm going to fuck you up when we get inside."* In an attempt to get away from him, I immediately ran inside, but he caught me before I could get away. He began dragging me throughout my apartment, across the carpet floor, causing rug burns on my arms. He then took a cordless phone and beat me against my face with it. I could feel the blood dripping from my forehead. After he beat me, he pulled down my pants and he fucked me like I was a prostitute he just paid for sex. I didn't fight him. I felt numb and dirty. I just laid in my bed while he was on me with tears rolling down the side of my face. Later in the night hours, he decided to take a shower. I took the opportunity to call my friend (*the one that he likes*). I told her he had beat me again, and I needed her to quickly hurry. I managed to quickly grab some clothing items and sneak out quietly without him knowing. I had only been at my friend's house a couple of hours when he began to call every hour, crying and begging me to come back home. My girlfriend convinced me again to go back with him because he loved me. I did go back the following day, but instead of going to work that day, I went to the police station to file a report against him. I thought that the law enforcement was going to help me, but I was wrong. The police officer asked me after I filed my complaint, "*What did you do to make him upset?*" He also asked me why I've never called the police when the domestic abuse allegedly happened the first time. Apparently, they thought I wasn't telling the whole truth. However, they did document my complaint. I assumed the bruises on my face were enough evidence. At this point, I don't know what to do or who to turn to. I thought that the law enforcement would arrest him. Instead, I was told to call the police to the home every time it happened so it could be documented and a possible arrest could be made. They did ask me if I wanted to file a restraining order against him, but I declined because I didn't feel I had their support. I do want him to leave my apartment, but I'm scared. I don't want him to find out that I went to the police. What should I do? He has isolated me from my friends and family. No one knows that I am going through this, and the only friend that knows about this is in the same predicament as me. So, she can't help me because she can't help herself. Please help me. I want to get out of this abusive relationship before he kills me.

Sincerely, Domestic Violence

Dear Domestic Violence,

Thank you for sharing your story. Admitting you are in an abusive relationship is the first step to getting the help that you need. There are more women like you that are currently in abusive relationships. They are afraid like you, and they believe they have no where else to turn, but that is untrue. There are groups and organizations that help women who are experiencing domestic abuse in their relationships and marriages. There are also women who never made it out in time. Unfortunately, their lives were taken away due to domestic abuse. If you want out of this relationship, you may have to leave with nothing but the clothes on your back. I understand that he resides in your apartment. But there are ways to get out of it. It's not too surprising that the law enforcement did not take your report seriously. Though there have been cases where women falsely accuse their boyfriends or husbands of a domestic assault, this is not the case for all women, such as yourself. It could have been misinterpreted or perceived as nothing so serious as to require an immediate response from them. Due to you not reporting in the past? Who knows. However, I could understand why it made you feel discouraged. Every person should feel confident in their law enforcement. This is why so many women keep quiet. Most women blame themselves or make excuses for their abusers. Women are not to blame for their abusers' pasts, emotional failures or for whatever love their abusers never received as children. You are not their mothers. Women must stop treating adult men like their sons. This is why you've accepted the abuse, because you felt badly about his childhood life and what he claims he went through. The first thing an abuser does is isolate you from your family and friends. Then he begins to control how you dress, where you go and what friends you hang around. This is why he liked your friend with six children. With six children, she couldn't go out and have a good time every weekend. She also is in an abusive relationship, and it has become normal to her. She believes that abuse is love. This is why she always convinced you to go back to your relationship. Your boyfriend kept you away from everyone you love, so he could have full control over you. He lied and told you that nobody loved you, and he belittles you as a woman because his agenda is to take away your self-esteem. He is really the one with the problems and the low self-esteem issues. There is nothing wrong with you. You just got into the wrong relationship. You have to leave, especially now that he told you he should have killed you. It's time for you to go. If you tell him you plan to leave him, he will not allow you to go without a fight. The only way to get away from him is to go into a domestic abuse shelter. Do not tell anyone, especially your friend (*the one that he likes*) about your plans to leave him because she would tell him everything. Below I'm going to provide you with numbers for a domestic abuse hotline. They will send someone out to meet you whereever you are, and they will take you to a secret location. No one, not even the police, will know your location. It's confidential for your safety. Please keep me informed of everything that happened, and PLEASE, GET OUT SMART and SAFELY!!!

Sincerely, Gurlé

The National Domestic Violence Hotline: For free help from trained advocates, call this hotline. To speak to someone in English call 1-800-799-7233, and to speak to someone in Spanish 1-800-787-3224. People can also text "LOVEIS" to 1-866-331-9474. More information can be found online at thehotline.org.

The National Sexual Assault Hotline: This hotline will connect callers to trained staff members who can help callers find help and resources with people in their area. Cal 1-800-656-HOPE (4673) or visit online at rainn.org.

Dear Gurlé,

I want to thank you for your help. I took your advice, and I reached out to someone at the *Domestic Violence* hotline. I must admit that I didn't seek help right away. I decided to give him another chance after my last letter to you. That was the biggest mistake that I've ever made in my life. We got back together, and everything appeared to be going better than great for three whole weeks. There were no arguments or any domestic altercations. I truly believed that he was making a change. He stopped cursing at me and calling me names. He was behaving like he did when we initially met. I was falling in love with him all over again. The sex was better, and we even discussed getting married. I was on a high note. We no longer argued when I said that I wanted to hang out with my girlfriends. I finally was able to visit with my mother, and he came along with me. I couldn't be happier. One night, while he was in the shower, I heard a buzzing sound. It wasn't my phone vibrating or his phone which was sitting on the nightstand next to my phone. I began looking around the room to investigate where the sound was coming from. I opened the closet door, and the vibration grew louder. I could hear the sound vibrating through his gym bag at the back of the closet. It was a cell phone that he hid away from me. By the time I located the phone it had stopped. I was curious. I wanted to know who was calling him. So, I pressed last caller on the phone, and a woman answered. She told me that she had been in a relationship with him for the past year and that she knew nothing about me. Before I could ask her any other questions, he got out of the shower. I took the phone and I hid it until he went to sleep. That night, I went through his phone, and I saw text messages from my friend with the six children in his phone. They were also seeing each other sexually. She shared with him all the things that I've told her in private. My mouth was on the floor. There were so many women's names in his phone that I couldn't keep count. I was angry, and I felt this was my chance to finally kick him out and end this relationship. I woke him up, and when he turned around to look at me, I was holding his cell phone in my hand. He asked me why the fuck I was going through his shit. He told me he didn't owe me any explanations, that he was a grown ass man, and that he wasn't my husband. Out of rage, I threw his cell phone in his face, and the phone hit his front teeth and chipped his tooth. He started fighting me like I was a grown ass man. We were so loud that the neighbors called the police, and they broke into my apartment and he was arrested! And YES, I filed charges against him, and he is not getting out of jail any time soon. He's looking at three to four years, especially since he punched an officer in his face. I also learned that I was not the first woman that he physically abused. The good news is that I am relocating to another state in one month. My job agreed to transfer me after I requested an emergency transfer. Although he's currently incarcerated, I still contacted the Domestic Violence Hotline to speak with them about counseling. As far as my friend (*the one that he likes*) she is pregnant with her seventh child by HIM!!!! Thank you for all your help and for taking the time to listen to my story.

Sincerely, Domestic Violence

Dear Domestic Violence,

Thank you for keeping me updated! I am so happy to hear how things turned around for you. I am saddened to learn that your friend was having a secret affair with him. The truth is she was never your friend. It's unfortunate that she may never come out of this abuse that she believes is real love. Not everyone wants to be saved. The goal is to save those that can be saved. Hopefully, one day, she will see her worth and seek help, too. I am glad to hear that you are seeking counseling. It will help you to move forward and heal, so that you will be able to identify healthy relationships. I wish you well on your new journey. You still have your entire life ahead of you. Just continue making the right decisions moving forward, and everything will continue to flow in the right direction for you. It may be best that you change your numbers and also reevaluate the company that you keep. I will make a small suggestion for you. Once you relocate, you don't have to share with everyone what you've been through, unless you're sharing your story as a testimony to help someone else. Best wishes!!

Sincerely, Gurlé

Dear Gurlé,

I have a *Competitive Friend* whom I've known for six years. I met her at one of my friend's get-togethers. She was invited by her husband's sister, who couldn't make the function at the last minute. We were seated at the same table and were the only two who didn't know everyone else. So, we just communicated with each other throughout that evening. We both learned that we had a lot in common. We exchanged numbers and our social media information. We promised to keep in touch with each other. She is thirty-eight years old and married to a professional athlete; together, they have a fourteen-year-old son. Over the next few years our friendship grew closer. I considered her to be my best friend, and I felt that I could trust her. I am a very private person. I usually don't connect well with other females. And I've always been against making new friends because of my past experiences. I've always been the type to keep the same group of friends in my life. But with her, I made an exception, and I let her in. One of the first things I learned about her is that she loves to talk about herself. Everything is always about her, her son, her husband, her career, her new bag, her shoes, ect. I've adjusted. I'm used to it now. Lately, I've noticed some changes in her behavior towards me. Whenever I shared any good things that were happening in my life, she didn't show the same genuine happiness for me as I have done with her. I met a guy, and he is the best thing that's happened to me in a very long time. We've been together over two years, and we are planning to get married. My boyfriend is a very generous man. One day, he surprised me with a Chanel designer bag (*because he knows how much I love Chanel*). A week after I shared with her what he did for me, she was carrying the same Chanel bag that my boyfriend had purchased for me. She "claimed" that her husband had purchased the Chanel bag for her months prior to me getting mine (*rolls eyes*). I didn't say anything to her about it, but I was feeling some kind of way. I told my boyfriend what happened, and he said that maybe she admired me and to take it as a compliment. I thought about it, and I felt he may be right until I shared with her that I was going to purchase the new Range Rover Sports Utility Vehicle as a Christmas gift to myself. One month before the Christmas holiday, she pulled up in front of my house with the exact vehicle that I told her I was going to purchase for myself. I was livid. All of a sudden she had amnesia. When I told her that was the same vehicle I shared with her I wanted to buy myself for Christmas, she "claimed" that she didn't remember. As badly as I wanted to tell her off, I didn't. I just sat back and I watched her closely. I admit she has more than I have financially. Her husband is a professional athlete, for goodness sakes. She can afford to purchase anything that she wants to. I have a great career. I am doing extremely well financially for myself. But I'm not married. I don't have a husband to take care of me. This is why I don't understand why she is secretly competing with me. I slowly began to distance myself away from her. I was no longer sharing with her the things that I was doing. Earlier, after we became cool, I introduced her to my circle of friends. I even invited her to come with me to a few of my friends' events as my guest. But she never introduced me to her other friends, and I was never invited to any of her friends' main events or parties. When we did connect with each other, it was always with me and my friends or just she and I hanging together. The people that she did introduce me to were people she felt held no value to her. So she didn't care about introducing those people to me. I always knew this about her, but I never let it stop me from being her friend because I was never in competition with her. But I guess she's been showing these competitive signs for a while. We were at my friend's birthday party one night, and I was wearing a pretty yellow outfit. I received so many compliments that night. During the party, I must have sat in something that caused a stain on the back of my pants. When I was dancing at the party, several people shared with me that I had a stain on my pants. She told me that she saw it earlier, but she thought that I knew the stain was there. I went into the ladies' room, and I thought to myself, *"She saw it, but she didn't tell me? What kind of friend is she?"* *"A Jealous Competitive Friend,"* I thought. But what really did it for me is when she told my boyfriend something that she "assumed" he didn't know about me. She told him this information in hopes of causing an issue within my relationship with him. But my boyfriend already knew this information about me. She had the audacity to ask him to keep it between them two. My boyfriend finally saw what I've been telling him about her all along. I haven't spoken with her in a month. She's been calling and texting me, but with friends like her who needs enemies? Our friendship was never genuine on her part, and I don't trust her at this point. It's one thing to admire someone, but she has taken it to another level. I don't want her knowing anything about me. I also feel strongly that she shared a secret that I told her in confidence with another friend that I introduced her to. I say this because I've also noticed the change in how that friend treats me now. I feel that she is trying to shatter my life. The crazy part is she talks more now with that friend than I do. That's just weird to me, and it makes me uncomfortable. I'm ready to move forward in my life. I don't dislike her, but I dislike her sneaky, conniving, jealous ways. Once I disconnect from her, I don't want her to have access to me or anyone attached to me, even my friends, whom she met through me. I know I cannot control my friends, but I will be upset if they continue to entertain her. Am I being childish? Do you feel that I am overreacting? How would you handle this situation?

Sincerely, Competitive Friend

Dear Competitive Friend,

There are a lot of people who can relate to your story. I don't think you are being childish about how you're feeling. But you also have to keep in mind that people are allowed to make their own choices. We all want to live in a world where the people we are loyal to are loyal to us, too. You introduced her to your friends because at that time you considered her to be your friend. But what happened between you and her has nothing to do with the friendships that she has developed with your friends outside of her friendship with you. In a perfect world, it would be great to have friends who show their loyalty for you in that way. Unfortunately, we don't live in a world where everyone views loyalty the same way as you do. However, there is nothing wrong with expressing to your friends your current feelings towards this person. But whatever you do, do not give your friends an ultimatum. You don't want to cause any division with them. If this person is competitive and untrustworthy as you've mentioned, your friends will eventually see this for themselves as well. The truth always gets revealed. I also agree that you should move on and sever all connections with this person. It is very dangerous to have a competitive friend in your life. That's worse than having an enemy that you don't know at all. When she disclosed something personal about you to your boyfriend, that was pure disrespect. That should have closed all doors for any future friendship with you. But despite what happened with your friendship with her, please leave room to develop new friendships with other women. Do not close the door to develop possible friendships in the future because of your past. Friendships are a great thing to have when formed with the right people. There are other women in the world who are like you that are sincere and loyal. Not every woman is jealous or in competition with the next girl. I don't want you to lose faith or trust in friendships. But we all have to eventually go through life lessons with people we call "friend." If the friends you've known the longest decide to continue their friendships with that person, you have to set your own boundaries and choose how you interact with them when she is around moving forward. I'm almost certain that your friends will support your feelings in the end, and their loyalty will be with you. But if not, you live and you learn in this stage of life who is really with you. This is what growing pains are all about. I wish you well.

Sincerely, Gurlé

"If you find one true friend in your life, hold onto them because true friends often don't come around twice in a lifetime."

– Caprice Lamor –

Dear Gurlé,

I am what most would consider a *Ride or Die* female. Some people consider most Ride or Die females to be fools, depending on the circumstances of their male partners. I am a happily married woman. I have been with my husband since high school. My husband had a very rough life growing up. He was raised by his maternal aunt who is like his mother. My husband never got a chance to meet his birth parents. They both are deceased. My husband's dream was to always own his own business company. He never liked the idea of having someone else tell him what to do. He was employed with a company for five years before he decided to leave and go full-time to build his own business company. I believe in my husband's vision one hundred percent, and I know that his hard work will pay off one day. This past year has been very hard for us financially. I have a full-time job, and I make sixty-five thousand dollars a year. But my income alone cannot cover our monthly bills. Our mortgage is three months behind in payments, and his car could be repossessed any day now. I had to swallow my pride and borrow money from my mother on three occasions and once from my oldest sister. We have a twenty-five-year-old son in college, and he is not receiving financial assistance. It has been very rough. Despite everything that is happening, I trust in my husband, and I will continue to stand by his side. However, my mother and sister are telling me that enough is enough. They say my husband is the man of the house, and it's his responsibility to handle the bills. My sister told our friends my business, and now everyone is talking. One of our close friends stated that females need to stop riding so much for these men because they're out here dying. I was very upset to learn that my business is being discussed in the streets. My husband is angry with my mother and sister, and he refuses to speak to them. Our circumstances weren't always this way. My husband sacrificed a lot, so I could complete college. There was a time that I wasn't working at all. My husband was providing for me, for his aunt who raised him, and he also did things for my mother. I have a good husband. He is a provider in my eyes. Although he's not working right now, he does all the cooking and the house chores. He's always treated me with respect, and he's working very hard to build his company, which will be up and running any day now. My mother and sister are making my husband out to be something that he is not. I will ride with my husband until the wheels falls off. I believe in him. I have a girlfriend who has everything. Her husband is rich, but she is unhappy. He doesn't treat her with respect or care for her the way that my husband cares for me. It's not always about money. I know that money is important to have – it is a necessity. But money doesn't make you happy. It may make certain individuals happy, but not me. The funny thing is my girlfriend always tells me that she wished that her husband treated her the way that my husband treats me. This is coming from a woman who has it all. I am beginning to regret going to my mother and sister for help. I really want to tell my mother how I feel, but I don't want to cause any more tension. I just need my mother and sister to know their boundaries. I know that I came to borrow money from them, but that doesn't give them the right to share my personal business or to speak against my husband. How can I handle this situation with my mother and sister? I don't believe that because I borrowed money from them both, they now have the right to be in my business. And it doesn't give them the right to judge my husband. Am I wrong for sticking by my husband's side? Do you feel that there should be limitations on how far a woman will ride or die for her spouse or partner? What advice can you give me because I'm beginning to feel stressed about everything. Please help?

Sincerely, Ride or Die

Dear Ride or Die,

Thank you for reaching out to me. Let me start off by saying, "For better, For Worse, For Richer, and For Poorer." Those were the vows that you took with your husband, not with your mother, sister or friends. You don't owe anyone an explanation. It doesn't matter how much money they've loaned you. It is a loan. I know that you have respect for your mother, but you have to set boundaries with your mother and sister. Your husband comes first, and you know the type of man he is to you and so does your family. They may never admit it to you, but they know that you have a good husband. To answer your question, I would never tell another woman what her limitations should be or how long she should ride or die for her significant other. We each know as women how much we are willing to compromise and give of ourselves for any man. What one woman may be willing to compromise, the next woman may not. But that doesn't give anyone the right to judge that woman, because she chooses to support her husband, or significant other, however she chooses. As you stated in your letter, you have a friend who is married to a wealthy man, but she is very unhappy. We live in a world where people believe that money, houses, cars and fame are the key to happiness when they're not. None of these possessions can love you in return. What happens if you fall ill? It doesn't matter how much money you have; your health is going to be all that matters to you. Yes, we all want to live rich, debt-free, travel-all-around-the-world kind of lives. And we also all want to experience real love. I agree that you should stick by your husband no matter what, especially if he believes in his dream and he is working hard towards it every day. Although he does not have a physical job, he is still working to build his own company. That is considered working. He's just not being compensated yet for his labor. But he will. You continue to support your husband, but most importantly, you have to respectfully put your mother and sister back in their

95

places. The last thing you want is to cause division in your own home. People will always talk and say what they want to say. You have to learn which battles to pick and choose. As soon as you get some extra money, pay back your mother and sister. If you can help it, find other resources to borrow from in the future if you really need the help. Do not discuss with others any further money issues or hardships between you and your husband, not even to your mother. Your mother will always be your mother, and she will always get the respect that she is owed. But you have to draw some boundaries, or it will cause issues, not only for your marriage, but between your husband and your family. Whatever happens, you continue to support your husband if that's what YOU chose to do. Your decisions will affect your life, not your mother's or your sister's. Thank you again for contacting me. Please keep me posted with what happens. I'm looking forward to hearing back from you.

Sincerely, Gurlé

Dear Gurlé,

I reached out to you a few months ago. I'm the *Ride or Die* woman. I just want to inform you that you were correct about everything that you stated. I've allowed my mother and sister for most of my life to have a lot of control over me, and I've always given them too much access to my marriage. I sat down with my mother, and I told her how I really felt about the way she spoke against my husband. I also let my sister know that my personal business was not her business to share with the world. I was very respectful with my words to the both of them, but I was also stern. I wanted them to understand that what I was saying to them was coming from a real place. After I told them how I felt, I politely paid them each back all of the money that I had borrowed, before handing them my husband's COMPANY card. Yes! The hard work and dedication have paid off. My husband found an investor that truly believes in his product, and in less than two months, my husband's company income crossed six figures, and it continues to climb. We are all caught up with our bills, and last week, we paid for our son's last semester in college. I am beyond ecstatic about everything that is transpiring and so quickly. My husband told me that his goal is for me to never have to work again, unless I chose to. He told me this is why he has been working so hard for me and our son. He thanked me for being his true rock and his Ride or Die. I am so glad that I didn't give up on my husband. One thing I've learned is that you may not always come into an establishment already built. Remember my girlfriend who I mentioned that is married to a wealthy man? Well, she divorced him. She is currently dating a chef. The chef has an apartment, not a house, and he drives a Buick, not a luxury car. But guess what. She is in love, and she said that he treats her better than any man has ever treated her in her life. Thank you again for everything, but most importantly for keeping it real with me.

Sincerely, Ride or Die

Dear Gurlé,

I'm *Homeless,* and I've been living in my car with my two children. I am embarrassed and ashamed. After I separated from my children's father, I was unable to handle the monthly bills. I was evicted from our apartment seven months ago, and we've been living in my car since that day. I didn't want to go to a shelter; I've heard so many horror stories about them. I have a thirteen-year-old daughter and an eight-year-old son. No one knows that we are sleeping in the car. I usually park behind Walmart or behind this church building every night when we rest. Those are the safest places. Every morning I drive to the nearest restaurant, and we take turns washing up there. I don't have anyone I can turn to, and I don't have any resources. My children's schools are beginning to suspect that something is going on because my son wore the same clothes three days in the row. I don't want to lose my children because I don't have a place to provide for them. I have a job and I make decent money, believe it or not. But I cannot afford to fully support my children and myself with my income alone. I don't qualify for welfare assistance because I make over the amount required to qualify for help or assistance which I don't understand. I feel that the system is set up for you to fail. I am doing all that I can do to save money, but it's hard and stressful on me and my children. I found a one-bedroom apartment, but because I have a son and a daughter the law requires me to have a bedroom for each child. They cannot share a room together. I am so depressed. We left our home state with my children's father because I believed that we were going to get married and build our life together. I gave up so much to be with him because I believed that we were going to be a family. The other day I just broke down and cried, and my children gave me the biggest hug and told me "*Mommy, we're going to be alright. God is going to help us.*" I really broke down. I should be consoling my children; they shouldn't be consoling me. I know that I'm going to get through this, and when I do, my children will never have to experience this again. I never saw my life this way. I've been thinking about what else I can do. I thought about sending my children to our home state to live with their godmother. She is like a mother to me. I know that she would help me out with my children. I would remain living here and save as much money as I could and send for my children later. I am also taking into consideration that their godmother is in her seventies. I don't want to put that strain on her. We lived next door to her when we lived in the same state. She's known my children since they were babies. She asked me if she could be both my children's godparent, and I couldn't say no to her. She used to care for them when I had to work late hours. She absolutely adores my children. The day that I told her we were moving out of the state, she cried. She has lived alone so long, and she has no family and no children of her own. Her husband died years ago. I want to reach out to her, but I don't want to inconvenience her at all. I also don't want to keep moving my children around in schools. I just need some direction on what to do. At this point, I don't have anywhere else to turn. Should I humble myself and call their godmother, or should I find another option? Please help. I am slowly losing my mind. Also, the address that I am using is a Post Office address, so I will be able to receive a response back from you.

Sincerely, Homeless

Dear Homeless,

I am sorry to learn that you and your children are homeless. I can only imagine the levels of stress and anxiety that you are feeling each day. This could be very overwhelming on any person with children. It is unfortunate that you didn't qualify for assistance because you made just a little above the requirement. There are so many people out here that are experiencing the same things right this moment. Hopefully, things will change to better help families that are in need. Just because a person's income is a certain amount doesn't mean they don't need assistance. Life is very expensive, especially when you are a single parent with growing children. To answer your question, I feel that you should humble yourself and call your children's godmother. You have nothing to lose but more to gain at this moment. Your children are familiar with her, and they grew up in that state all their lives prior to your move. I truly feel that if you reach out to her, she would be more than happy to help out. If you have to move as well, do what you need to do. It's about your children right now. You can no longer continue living in a vehicle with your children. Eventually, your children's schools will find out or Child Services will be notified, and things will turn for the worse. If you have someone you can call, reach out to her, and tell her the truth about what's currently happening. If she lives alone, she will love to have someone staying with her. I know that you stated you don't want to stay in the shelter, but I'm going to provide you with some places that you can call for shelter. Not all shelters are bad. Perhaps you can look up the websites at a public library. And please feel free to share them with anyone that needs them. Please contact me back and let me know what you decided to do. I look forward to hearing from you soon.

Sincerely, Gurlé

The Salvation Army: Go to this website to see the resources and support provided to people in need. In order to find a location near you, go to "Contact Us." To find a shelter near you, go to "What We Do," and click "Homeless Shelters." www.salvationarmyusa.org

Women's Shelters: Visit this site to see an extensive list of women's shelters nationwide: www.womenshelters.org.

Dear Gurlé,

I contacted you last month regarding being *Homeless* with children and living in my vehicle. Well, I took your advice, and I humbled myself and reached out to my children's godmother. She was so happy to hear from me. I told her everything, and before I could say anything else, she said that my children and I were welcome to live with her as long as needed. I broke down and cried tears of joy over the telephone. It was such a relief from a long seven months of stress and worry. My children are even more excited because they get to move back to their old neighborhood with their friends. I spoke with my job, and they are willing to give me a transfer, so I could continue working when I move back to our original state. I signed both of my children out of their schools, and we are driving back home this weekend. This has been a tough journey. But I am glad that we are getting a second chance to get it together. I just want to thank you for taking the time to listen. I needed that more than anything. I feel like a ton of weight has been lifted off my shoulders. But most importantly, my children will be safe. Thanks again for everything.

Sincerely, Homeless

Dear Gurlé,

I am thirty-four years old, and I just received the worst, depressing news of my life. I have a *Sexually Transmitted Disease.* I have been in a relationship with my fiancé for three years prior to us getting engaged earlier this year. He is the third man in my entire life that I have ever been with sexually. Last year, before we were engaged, I found out that he was cheating on me with his coworker. They were having sexual relations before he and I ever met, but they were never a couple. It was more of a "Friends with Benefits" relationship. I knew about her before we started dating, but he told me that the sexual relations between them were over. We went through a bad breakup after I found out he had been with her. On Valentine's Day, which is also my birthday, he surprised me with this huge proposal. The morning of my birthday, he called me and he managed to convince me to have dinner with him at this banquet hall. At the time, we had been apart for about five months. I questioned him about the location because it didn't make sense, but he told me that they were serving dinner for Valentine's Day couples, and he had made special reservations. Okay, I fell for it. When we arrived at the banquet hall, the parking lot was full so we had to park on the street. We walked inside the banquet hall room, and all I heard was *"Surprise!"* Now, I'm just standing there trying to process what the hell was going on. I began to recognize my family and friends in the crowd. Of course, I'm still trying to do the math. I see birthday and Valentine's Day balloons, and everyone was dressed really nice. Everyone was taking pictures and recording us. I just stood in place looking around like Dorothy from the Wizard of Oz (*in a strange, confused atmosphere*). I turned around to look at him, and he was on one knee holding a three carat diamond ring. I just cried and cried. It all felt so surreal. Everyone was screaming and running towards us with their phones as they took more pictures. In the moment, everyone was asked to quiet down by the DJ, but you could still hear the excitement in the room. The song "Bended Knee" by Boyz II Men started to play as he softly sang along with the music. I stood there shaking. As the music softened, he took my right hand and spoke the most beautiful, heartfelt words to me. He told me that he was in love with me, and that he has never loved a woman the way that he loved me. He started crying and so was everyone present in the room. He told me that I challenged him in ways that he has never been challenged, and I helped him to become a better man. He told me that he couldn't live life without me any longer, and he asked me to be his wife. I said yes, and we kissed for the first time since we had broken up. It was the best night of my life. My two best friends and family were there. His best friend and family were there as well. My mother didn't come because she never liked him, and she's always told me that she never trusted him. I was bothered at first that my mother wasn't there, but I knew after she learned we were engaged, that she would change her opinions about him. Everything was going excellent between us for the next several months. I actually trusted him again. I didn't have any doubts or felt a strong sense of woman's intuition or anything. I felt that it was finally happening. We continued to live in our separate apartments until both of our leases were up that fall. But I had the key to his place, and he had the key to my place as well. The love making between us was so passionate and intense that I would cry as we were making love. I told him to promise me that he would never hurt me like that again. And he promised me. I couldn't have been more in love with him. Six months after the proposal, he had to leave town for work business. He has a really great, high paying job. I decided that I was going to stay at his apartment the night that he left for his trip. We made love, said our goodbyes, and he left for his business trip. Around midnight, his house phone started ringing. He never used his house phone, so I just ignored it. I thought nothing about it. The house phone rang two more times, and by the third time I answered, *"Hello?"* then click. The person hung up. I went back to bed and just as I was about to lay back down, the phone rang again. This time I made sure I got to it before it stopped ringing. *"Hello?"* Nothing. *"Hello."* I heard this soft woman's voice, *"Is this* (she said my fiancé's name) *home?"* I said, *"Yes it is, and how may I help you?"* The woman on the other end just chuckled and murmured, *"He ain't shit."* I said, *"Excuse me?"* The woman on the phone introduced herself as his fiancé. I told her that I was his fiancé. There was silence. She told me that she was parked in front of his building in a champagne Lexus. She said that she felt that something wasn't right, so she drove to his apartment. I looked outside the balcony's front window and saw her sitting inside her vehicle. So, I did what any woman would have done. I invited her to come inside, so we could have a mature conversation about it. She knocked on the door. I answered. When I first saw her, I couldn't understand what he saw in her. Physically, she definitely was not his type at all. I know the type of women he likes. She was the total opposite of me. We sat down in the living room, and when she looked at me, she just broke down and cried. She shook her head in disbelief. She said that she and my fiancé met two years ago when she went on a girls trip with her friends to Cancun, Mexico. She told me the same night she met him they had a one night stand. She stated she had never done anything like that before, but there was something different about him that made her feel secure. He was very charming. As she's talking, I'm sitting there boiling inside, because he and I were together during that time. I knew that she was telling the truth because I remembered when he went away with his friends to Cancun, Mexico two years ago. She said that they exchanged numbers, and he told her that he was in a *"very complicated situation,"* referring to me. She said that he told her he wanted to get to know her better, so they agreed to hook up again when they returned home from their trip. She told me she knew about me from the beginning, but he always made her believe that I was stalking him and begging him to stay with me. He told her that I was needy and had a lot of drama in my life. I couldn't believe what I was hearing. All the lies he told her! I was in disbelief. She told me she knew he and I had broken up, but she assumed it was because he finally ended the relationship with me. She said she didn't know we were back together or about his coworker at that time. She told me that he proposed to her one night when it was the two of them at a quiet dinner. She said she often spent nights at his apartment and she even purchased a painting (*as she pointed*) that was hanging on his wall. She said they broke up two months ago, but he never took the ring back from her. She had learned that he was cheating on her with some girl that he met at a club. This was too much. But I wanted to know everything, so I just let her do all the talking. She told me that he had been calling her everyday since they had broken up; he was begging her to take him back. He told her that he loved her and he wanted her to be the mother of his children. He also met her parents, and they absolutely love him. She stated that she knew he was up to something when his phone calls just stopped two weeks ago. I must admit this woman spoke very properly. I could tell that she was raised with morals and values. She never raised her tone or appeared to be angry with me. In most cases like this, women often blame each other, instead of the man. She appeared to have it all together. She works at a law firm, and she owns her own condo. Both of her parents are lawyers. Now I could understand what he saw in her. She told me that after she learned about the girl from the club, she later found out that he was also cheating on her with a twenty-one-year-old Stripper. The twenty-one-year-old girl works at a strip club that he hangs out at with his work buddies after hours. I just sat there thinking to myself, "*How the hell did I miss all of this?*" The sex really had me blinded. She said she went to her doctor one week ago, and she learned that she contracted a Sexually Transmitted Disease. She said immediately after she found out, she called my fiancé because she had not been with anyone other than him. She knew that my fiancé gave it to her. She told me he refuses to take her calls, and he keeps sending her to his voicemail. She cried, but I stood strong

106

like a trooper. I refused to let her see me cry. I thanked her for telling me what I needed to know and she left. After she left, I sat in the living room for three hours just crying. I knew that this woman had no reason to lie. He was a cheater and I've always known that he was. The following morning, I left his apartment, and I tried to figure out what to do next. I was frightened after she stated she contracted a Sexually Transmitted Disease. I've never had any issues with my body, so I assumed that she could have contracted it from someone else. I don't know. I guess I just tried to convince myself of that. I decided to get a check-up that week, and when I received the report from my doctor that I had a Sexually Transmitted Disease, I freaked out. She was telling the truth. That night he returned back from his business trip. I told him that I was going to meet him at his apartment. I arrived to his apartment, but I wasn't alone. I brought Champagne Lexus with me, his other fiancé. When he walked into the living room and saw us both sitting there together, he looked as if he had seen a ghost. I said, "*So, this is what it comes down to?*" He began pleading with me, telling me that he loves me, and that he never loved her. Champagne Lexus just cried. She couldn't take anymore and she left. I gave him the paper from my doctor, and he looked at me and said that he was sorry. He didn't know that I would get it, too. I said to him, "*Wait . . . so, let me get this straight. You knew your ass was infected with an STD, and you still engaged in sexual activities with me? Smh . . . You felt that comfortable with me sucking your dick knowing your dick was contagious? How disrespectful of your selfish ass!! You told me you were STD free!! Wow . . . But you know what? I blame myself. I should have never allowed you back into my life. I never make any promises, but I promise you this: I AM DONE WITH YOU!! Fuck you and everything attached to you!!*" I took my engagement ring off my finger. YES I DID, because it was all a lie, and I threw it at the wall as hard as I could. I went to leave and he grabbed me as he cried and pleaded for me not to leave him. I told him that it was over. He would never have me or see me again. I was so focused that I didn't have time to become emotional. He struggled with me for almost an hour before he finally let me leave his apartment. I knew once I walked out of that door it was over for good. It's been eight months since that happened. Since then, he has called me, sent me flowers and gifts, but I just ignore him. I'm now looking at my life thinking, *"Why me?"* I've never been promiscuous. I now have this stigma attached to me for the rest of my life. I feel so dirty and more embarrassed than anything. How can I move forward in another relationship? I am only thirty-four years old. Will I be able to have children? Will I ever get married now? I have friends who are promiscuous, and this never happens to them. The thought makes me angry. I am always the careful one, and I take pride in caring for myself. Is God punishing me? This has to be a mistake. One of my close friends also just learned that her husband gave her an STD. She confided in me, and she is devastated. I haven't shared with anyone what happened to me except with her, because I trust her, and she is going through the same thing. The difference is she is married, and she is staying with her husband. The sad part is her husband continues to cheat with other women, knowing that he has an STD. And he has even accused his wife of giving him the STD. Why do men do this to good women? There are so many more women going through this as well. And they are all embarrassed to say it because it is humiliating. I don't know what to do. How am I going to live life now? He took my life away from me. He lied. The thought of me having to tell the next man that I date (*if it ever happens again*) is making me sick. I have been in the bed feeling depressed for months. I don't go anywhere, and I don't communicate with my friends as much. I don't feel like myself, and I'm just in a really dark place. We live in a very cruel world, and I don't want anyone to know because people judge you, and they say hurtful things. What should I do? I feel so lost, confused and scared.

Sincerely, Sexually Transmitted Disease

Dear Sexually Transmitted Disease,

Thank you for being so transparent and open about what happened to you. I am sorry to hear what's happened. The sad truth is there are many women of all ages going through this right now. No one wants to get this kind of medical report from their doctor, especially when they are in a devoted marriage and can count the number of their sexual partners on one hand and they are not promiscuous. I can understand why this may be embarrassing to you. We do live in a world where people are very cruel and insensitive towards people who have contracted STD's. People need to understand that there are mothers, wives, doctors, teachers, girlfriends, fiancés, pastors of all races, beliefs and cultures that have contracted an STD from their husbands, boyfriends or fiancés who they loved and trusted. Just because a person learns that another individual contracted an STD, doesn't mean that the person is dirty or doesn't have morals, values or standards. I can only imagine what you are going through. But I will tell you this. Your life is not over. Speak with your doctor to see if what you have contracted is curable. Also, learn about better ways to naturally treat what you are carrying. If this is making you feel depressed, go speak with a counselor and get it all out. You will find someone in the future that will love you and care for you no matter the outcome. You will get married and have the family that you've always desired. But YOU have to believe this for yourself. It's not over for you. You are young, strong and beautiful. Don't allow a doctor's report to take away your life. As long as you are walking this earth, you still have a purpose to fulfill. I know that you are angry with your ex-fiancé, but you have to forgive him and let it go. I know it sounds impossible, but you have to do this for you. I have a strong feeling that you are going to come out of this a winner. And the next time that you visit with your doctor, he's going to tell you that you are fine. Stay positive and speak good things into your atmosphere. You don't have to exchange pity notes with your close friend who is also going through the same thing. Try not to focus so much on what the doctor reported to you, and focus on the good things. Life is still beautiful, and life is still going to reward you with everything that the universe said belongs to you. Whatever happens, be honest with the next person that enters into your life. But only share if you know the relationship is becoming more serious. You don't have to walk around holding up a sign stating, *"I have an STD."* Now that would make a person depressed. Again, stay strong. I know that things will work out for you. Thank you for sharing. I wish you the best.

Sincerely, Gurlé

CDC-INFO (formerly known as the CDC National STD Hotline) 1-800-CDC-INFO (1-800-232-4636) | 1-888-232-6348 TTY

- Available 8am-5pm Mon-Fri (Eastern time), in English and Spanish, counselors are available to answer questions about personal health issues, including HIV and other STD's. An online zip code tool for finding local HIV and STD testing locations are available at www.hivtest.org and www.findstdtest.org.

If you are sexually active, it's recommended that you get tested at least once a year. Here is a guide from the CDC on how often you should get tested based on your age, partner preference, and other situations:

- All adults and adolescents from ages 13 to 64 should be tested at least once for HIV.
- All sexually active women younger than 25 years should be tested for gonorrhea and chlamydia every year.

Women 25 years and older with risk factors such as new or multiple sex partners or a sex partner who has an STD should be tested for gonorrhea and chlamydia every year.

- All pregnant women should be tested for syphilis, HIV, and hepatitis B starting in early pregnancy. At-risk pregnant women should also be tested for chlamydia and gonorrhea starting early pregnancy. Testing should be repeated as needed to protect the health of mothers and their infants.

If you think you have been exposed to an STD, below is a recommended guideline for when to get tested by the CDC.

- Chlamydia: get tested 1-5 days after possible exposure.
- Gonorrhea: get tested 2-6 days after possible exposure.
- Syphilis: get tested 3-6 weeks after possible exposure.
- Herpes I and II: get tested 4-6 weeks after possible exposure.
- Hepatitis B: results may be detected 3 weeks after exposure, but for most accurate results get tested 6 weeks after possible exposure.
- Hepatitis C: get tested 8-9 weeks after possible exposure.
- HIV: get RNA test 9-11 days after exposure and antibody test 1-3 months after exposure.

Please know that all STD testing is confidential and private. Clinics and doctor offices guarantee complete patient confidentiality and privacy and will aim for you to feel as comfortable as possible. However, healthcare providers are required to make a report if they believe you are at a significant risk or harm by either yourself or someone else.

Planned Parenthood U.S. National Sexual Health Hotline: Planned Parenthood provides counseling for STDs, pregnancy and other sexual health issues. To contact Planned Parenthood, call 1-800-230-PLAN (7526). They are available Mon-Fri or as local center hours permit – call to be directed to a Planned Parenthood near you.

Dear Gurlé,

I'm what you call a *Loyal Friend.* When I am down with you, I am down with you. Loyalty means everything to me, and for the most part, my closest friends reciprocate the same loyalty. I have five girlfriends that I've known since elementary school; we're all in our early thirties. We consider each other best friends. We're always there to support each other during birthdays, holidays, special events and crucial times in our lives. Each one of us has our own personality, and none of us are quite alike. It's amazing how long we've remained friends. I don't want to say my friends' names in my letter, so I'm going to refer to each of them by their zodiac signs or another name. That way as I explain, you will know which friend I am referring to in the letter. My friend Leo is very book smart. She achieved her masters degree by the time she was twenty-eight. She likes to be the center of attention. But she is not the one to get into a debate with, because she will argue with you until she wins. My friend Virgo is a perfectionist. She looks at everything in such a deep way. She believes strongly in horoscopes and astrology. Another thing I can say, she is a very hard worker. She didn't attend college, but she started her own business. She is truly a go getter. Between Virgo and Leo, they both feel they are the smartest of everyone. Word of advice, never talk about Virgo's man or anyone she loves. You've been warned. My friend Aquarius is very intelligent. She sometimes may come off with an nonchalant attitude or may act like she could care less attitude. Truth is, she does what she feels is best for her. But she loves God. She grew up in a church all of her life, but when she turned twenty she turned Catholic. By the time she was twenty-two she turned Muslim. When she turned twenty-four, she went back to church and said that Christianity is where she belonged. Like I've mentioned, Aquarius has her own mind, and she pursues her own freedom. She refuses to be controlled by anyone. However,

113

Aquarius brings so much balance to our group of friends. But please, don't tell the others that I said that. My friend Taurus is what you consider the ride or die type of friend. She is real, and she tells you how she feels without sugar coating anything. Taurus is into real estate. She also has her own company. She is building her own empire for herself and her family. Our other friend, I will call her Sunny instead of using her zodiac sign. Sunny is the only one out of all of us who has children. She has three children with two different men. Sunny gives her heart to the wrong people, and she is very indecisive. She recently started community college, what some might call a little late, because during our sophomore and junior year of high school she had two sons, nine months apart. She had her third son two years ago. This is why it took her so long to go back to school. She is currently taking classes to become a medical assistant. Sunny is also a manager at Target. I will tell you more about her, but let me tell you about me. I am the friend who is the most rounded out of all the girls. I am the mediator and the one who they trust the most. They all come to me about each other and often times, I feel caught in the middle. There are days that I feel that I am the glue that's holding us all together. I am a college graduate. I am doing extremely well for myself financially. I am saving for my first home, which I am looking to purchase by early next year. The truth is I know all the secrets in this group. As I've mentioned, they all come to me and tell me things they would never share with each other. I love all my girls. They are like the sisters I've never had. But the ladies and I are having issues with how to deal with our other friend, Sunny. Whenever Sunny invites us to come over to her home for functions or gatherings we no longer attend. The last time we were at her house it was filthy and disgusting. The bathroom was worse than a public restroom. Once, we all made up an excuse to leave early because we all had to use the restroom, and we didn't feel comfortable using hers. In her home, she had piles of dishes in her kitchen sink and dried up juice stains were over the countertops and floor. She blamed her children for the house not staying clean and for their roach problems. On top of that, she prepares food for her guests to eat with all that filth happening. Her family doesn't seem to have any issues eating the food that Sunny prepares. But we do. So, we usually tell her that we had dinner prior to coming over. This way we don't hurt her feelings. One of the things I admire most about our friendships is that we all take pride in caring for ourselves. Sunny has never been as tidy or clean as the rest of us. But we've always loved and accepted her for her. When she began having children, that's when we each realized how unsanitary she could be. Her children are never clean. I get that boys are rough, but what excuse is there for her two-year-old son to be unclean. A mutual friend of ours told me that Child Protective Services were called on her several times, due to a concern about her children's appearances when they go to school. Sunny has never disclosed this with any of us. She is currently in a relationship with a guy (*he is not the biological father to any of her children*). She caters to him more than her own children, and he recently moved in with her. He doesn't work and he is unsanitary as well. This is the third guy this year that she's allowed to move into her apartment. It has become so bad between her and the other girls that I'm the only one who still communicates with her. Sunny and Taurus got into a terrible argument one day. Taurus told her that she was nasty as hell and that she needs to take care of her children and stop putting these men first. Aquarius tried to keep things calm. Sunny then cursed at Taurus and Aquarius, who only was trying to help keep the peace between the two. I don't know how Virgo and Leo became involved in the argument. The next thing I know I'm caught in the middle trying to keep them all from fighting Sunny. I love my friends, and I don't want to see our friendships fall apart, but I have to agree with the other ladies. Sunny is not taking care of her children. She feeds them junk food and allows them to drink juice all day. I have never seen them eating fruit or drinking water. Sunny doesn't clean or cook, but she makes sure that her hair and nails are always done, and she wears the latest fashions. I want to tell her the truth about what I am feeling without hurting her feelings. But I don't know if this would end our friendship. I have remained a Loyal Friend to these five ladies since the fifth grade. I don't want to turn my back on Sunny, and I want us all to eventually work it out. What should I do? Help?

Sincerely, Loyal Friend

Dear Loyal Friend,

Thank you for reaching out to me. Your letter was very interesting. I feel as if I know all of your friends because you described them all so well. It's a blessing to have friends that you look to as a sister. I could hear in your letter how much each of these ladies mean to you. You stated that you are a "Loyal Friend," and that's what you've been to them in their lives. So continue being the Loyal Friend. I believe it's all about how you approach a situation. A person should be sensitive when it comes to certain topics, especially when children are involved. None of you ladies have children. So none of you could understand what your friend, Sunny, may be going through as a single, young mother with three sons. You stated that Sunny had her first son when she was just a sophomore in high school, and she had her second son during her junior year. She was still a child herself. I don't know her family dynamics because you never shared that in the letter, but it sounds to me that she didn't have any adult guidance growing up. If you or the ladies are truly her friends and you care about the welfare of her children, you should have an open dialogue with her without making her feel that you are demeaning who she is as a person or a mother. When an individual is use to being and living a certain way all of their life, especially when no one has ever told them that they were doing it the wrong way, of course they will become defensive. Because all of this time, they have been doing things one way, and now suddenly people want to show them the correct way to do it. It could be very confusing to a person with her thinking mentality. I am not saying that Sunny's parenting and unsanitary habits are validated. But if you were never taught right, how can you do right? Due to you being the friend that all the ladies confide in the most, I believe that if you sat her down and spoke with her about your observations and your concerns in a genuine way, she would be receptive to what you had to say to her. I strongly feel that once you speak with

117

her, she will open up to you even more about her childhood. And you will understand her better, as well as be able to know how to help her. I also believe that she will get it together and you ladies will all work out your differences. Friends are very hard to find. When you have a group of friends that have been in your corner for years, whom you know you can count on, don't allow anything that can be fixed destroy your foundation. Sunny needs you ladies as her friends more than ever now. You guys have been friends all these years for a reason. I don't feel that I would ever stop speaking with my friend over her sanitation issues or my concerns for her children's hygiene. If the children were being physically abused, that's another discussion. But in this case, she makes sure that her children eat, although fast food is not the best option. Have a talk with Sunny, and after you speak with her, if she is not receptive to what you are saying as her friend, there is nothing more you can do. One thing I do know is that anything that is real must be tested. And if your friendships are genuine like you stated in your letter, then you ladies should be able to work it out. She needs your help. Don't turn your back unless she tells you to walk away. I hope everything goes well, and thank you again for reaching out.

Sincerely, Gurlé

Dear Gurlé,

I am a *Woman of God.* I gave my life to God when I was fifteen years old. I grew up in church my entire life. Growing up, I had to attend Sunday services whether I wanted to attend or not. As I became older in age, I turned to God for everything. I talked with God, and I prayed to God every day. A lot of my friends thought that I was weird. They didn't quite understand my spiritual relationship with God, because they didn't have one with Him. But for whatever reason, God kept me protected, and his favor was always over my life. I met my husband, who is in ministry, when we were twenty years old. We got married on my mother's birthday, September 24th; I was twenty-four. We have been married twenty years, and I must admit that I am very happy with my marriage. But I have a confession to make. I have been struggling this past year with myself, with God, and just life in general. The average person would look at my life and say, *"Girl you are blessed! What are you complaining about?"* I have the typical things that most women desire, but there are times that I don't feel so blessed. There are times when I don't want to pray or talk to God. There are times that I don't have faith and I have doubt. I get tired of people coming to me like I am God, as if I have all the answers. They pull on me for encouragement, prayer and guidance when I don't know which direction that I am going in myself at times. I know that God is real. I know this to be true. But I'm still human. I hurt like everyone else hurts. Just because I am a Woman of God, people feel that I don't have the right to get upset or be frustrated with people, too. So, because I am a Woman of God, I am not allowed to dance or sing to other music, besides religious music? Or have fun? I am not allowed to like fashion designers or red bottoms? I am not allowed to wear a dress suit because it's more stylish, yet still appropriate? Or do I need to wear a big hat and oversized clothing in order to appear respectful in my church attire? I am not allowed to dislike a person's demeanor, because I am supposed to be "holy" in their eyes? Well, I am not holy. I am human with flaws and many imperfections. Yes, I get tired of people, too. It's even worse in the church my husband pastors. The church members watch my every move to determine if I am "acting" like the Woman of God I should be. What the people of God fail to understand is that God is not seeking "actors" to play roles in His Kingdom. He is seeking real people with sincere hearts. Listen, there are days I don't want to be bothered with my husband. Yes, I said it! There are days that I don't like him or his bad habits. He has a bad habit of leaving the toilet seat up, and one night I fell in the toilet bowl. Just because I don't like my husband some days, doesn't mean that I don't love him. I am head over heels in love with him. But I am human. Having God in a person's life doesn't make them perfect. I get tested daily and tempted in my spirit like anyone else, especially in my workplace. There are days the old me, back from my street days, wants to come out and lay hands on some people. And I don't mean in a biblical way. But do I ever act out those feelings? No. The point that I am making is that Women of God go through things, too. We are not as strong as everyone thinks that we are all the time. We have our weak moments, and we have our moments where we do fall. I'm just overall exhausted from the constant fake smiling, the fake *"God bless you sister,"* the early and late calls for prayers and just church people all together. Please do not judge me. I'm just releasing out loud. I am certain I may not feel this way tomorrow. But today is just that day for me. I am usually positive and quick to speak well into someone's day. I am usually quick to pray against any demonic attacks. But lately, I've just been feeling defeated. I know there is more to me than this. My husband doesn't comprehend the place I'm in right now. There are some things that I need as a woman that he is unable to provide for me. I guess I just need someone to talk to that understands where I am right now. I need another woman who won't judge me after I've shared my most personal feelings or life details. We all need that someone, every woman does. I recognize that in some churches, Godly women are very competitive with one another. They form cliques according to the person's popularity, and sometimes the people worship their head leaders more than they worship their God. I just don't want to remain in this place, this feeling that I have today. I want to continue doing the work that God placed me on this earth to do. I just need to learn to rest. How do I do that and still be who everyone looks at me to be for them? I feel like I've burned myself out, and I don't know how to truly recover. I am human, too, and I don't always feel like being what everyone wants me to be all the time. What advice can you give me? I don't know who else to turn to. I can't even pray right now.

Sincerely, Woman of God

Dear Woman of God,

Thank you for being so honest and real in your letter. I admire your authenticity on this matter. There are many churchgoers that are quick to judge another individual. Yes, you are human; not one person on this earth is perfect. And no persons should ever hold anyone, such as their pastors, bishops, prophets, evangelists, priests, deacons, or the Pope, on the level that only God should be placed on. You are absolutely correct, and you have the right to have those humanly feelings that God placed inside of you. You should never feel the pressure to be to others what you are unable to be to yourself at times. Each believer has to seek God for themselves if they desire to have their own personal relationships with Him. They have to learn to pray for themselves and believe God for their own miracles. Please understand that we've all experienced being in a place where we just need our "don't want time." We don't want to be bothered. We don't want anyone to ask us for help, yet alone advice. We don't even want to be bothered with our spouses, children, family members, friends, or our coworkers. It's not just you who feels these things, too; it's women in general. Every woman on this planet has felt this at some point in her life, especially when she hits a milestone in age when she wonders if she could do better or if she may not be doing everything quite right in her life. I just need you to understand that it is okay to have those emotions from time to time. If God wanted you to have all of the answers, what would you need Him for? He created you to need and look to Him for everything. God wants you to come to Him even when you are hurt, angry, frustrated, feeling judged, used or confused. Just don't allow those feelings to consume you and keep you in those dark places for too long. You are entitled to pout, stomp and cross your arms like a little child to your God. But you were not designed by Him to be defeated or to stay knocked down for long periods of time. You just have to find your balance. If you are mentally and spiritually drained, you cannot take every person's phone call when they are in need of prayer. You cannot give more of yourself to individuals that are constantly pulling on you for guidance when you are asking God to guide you during those same moments. Give and pour of yourself when you are completely FILLED, not when you are near EMPTY. It's okay to send some people to voicemail and then check back with them a few days later when your mind is much clearer. It's okay to tell your spouse that you just need a day or two to shut down to recuperate. It's okay. Why? Because you are human. God already knows what you can and cannot handle. God even rested Himself on the seventh day in the book of Genesis. So, learn to rest. But most importantly, continue to keep God first in your life. Even when you are going through these moments, keep Him above all things. God has given you strength, and He has kept you even during the times you couldn't keep yourself. God knows your heart. He also understands that you desire friendships with people that you can relate to. But it's unfortunate there is a lot of division inside of churches today. The great thing about this is God will only judge you according to your own actions and thoughts, not according to anyone else's. Just continue to allow your light to shine. And those days when you grow weary and tired, you do have someone that you can turn to and call your friend. He's been there with you all of your life. That person is God. I am glad that you trusted me enough to share your story. But I recommend that you continue seeking God for answers and continue doing the work within you. Again, when you grow tired, tell Him all about it. Learn to rest not just in Him, but in you, too. We all need a moment of silence in our lives, to breathe, to think, to meditate and to reflect. And it's okay. You are human and you will be okay. I know God has you in His hands. Thank you again for reaching out to me. I wish you the best.

Sincerely, Gurlé

Dear Gurlé,

I am twenty-three years old and in a very dark place. I don't have anyone to turn to. Lately, I've been having *Suicidal Thoughts.* Since the break-up with my boyfriend, I haven't been the same. We were together since we were fifteen. He was my first everything. I am in such a dark and gloomy place. He doesn't want to be with me anymore. He told me that we were too young to continue being so serious. He's about to go off to college, and he wants to be free to see other girls. I cried and begged him to not break up with me. He told me that I was beginning to scare him, and this is why it was best that we broke apart. His mother is so happy that he broke up with me. I hate that bitch. She never liked me. She probably convinced him to end our relationship. Lately, I've just become so obsessed with him. I wasn't this way when he and I were together. But when we broke up, I turned into his stalker. I drive past his house at night to see if he is home. I even hacked into his voicemail, and I figured out his password to his Instagram and Twitter accounts. While stalking his Instagram, I learned that he DMs a lot with a girl we graduated with from high school. She wrote in his direct message, *"I've always liked you."* His response was, *"And I've always found you to be very attractive."* I thought, *"Oh really?"* I read further through his messages, and I was so furious when I read that they were meeting up for a movie date. So, I immediately called him and confronted him about what I found out, and he called me psychotic. So, now I'm psychotic? Okay, then I'll show him psychotic. I drove to his house, and I slashed his tires. I know I was wrong, but I was hurt. Since that day, he has changed his number, and he has blocked me from his Instagram and Twitter. I called his house to try to make amends with him, and his mother had the audacity to try to give me some advice. That bitch needs to stay the hell out of my way. It's all her fault. He is the only person that has ever understood me. We used to do everything together and now, just like that, he doesn't want me anymore. I can't live without him. I love him so much. I need him in my life. The other day, after I found out he was dating the same girl, I held my mother's gun to my head. But my younger sister knocked on my door before I could pull the trigger. I hurried and put the gun away before my sister could see it. My mother has no idea that I took her gun from her secret location that I'm supposed to know nothing about. But I always knew she had a gun and where it was locked away. My mother uses the same passcode all the time; it wasn't hard to figure out. I was going insane. I must have called his parents' home a hundred times before he finally answered the phone. He was calm. He didn't raise his voice, and he didn't sound agitated with me. He told me that he loved me and that he would always care for me, but I need to seek help and that the type of help I need he couldn't provide. I was in disbelief about what he was saying to me. The one guy that I had loved since I was fifteen years old? What went wrong? I have never been this person that I've become today. He caused me to be this way. A few days later, I received a restraining order from the sheriff's office. I was numb. I thought this was all a nightmare, but I wasn't asleep. Since that day, I've locked myself in my bedroom; it's been three weeks. I've been in my bed crying and feeling down and depressed. I don't know who I am without him. No one gets me, not even my mother. My mother is so far up my sister's ass she wouldn't notice me if I shaved all my hair off my head. My mother never noticed me. But he did. He noticed that I was a great painter and that when I smiled that one dimple would pop up on the right side of my chin. He's always told me that I was special and that I could become anything I wanted to be. I just want to die. I don't want to live without him. There is no other reason to live my life if he cannot be a part of it. How could he just move on and date other girls after being with me and loving me? You don't know what it's like to lose someone that you truly love. He was my entire life. If he would have told me that I was too clingy, I would have given him more space. Now I'm crazy? I need help? And I am being ordered by the law to keep away from him. My father killed himself, and my father's mother, killed herself. Now I am having those same thoughts. I visualized myself dead inside of a casket, and he was crying. He was broken and hurt. I was glad that he was hurting without me. That's exactly how I want him to feel, remorseful. I want him and my mother to hurt and to feel all my pain. I want them to feel guilty if I kill myself, so they can deal with the guilt for the rest of their lives. No one sees my pain, and right now I can't feel myself. I am writing you in hopes that you can help me see the light, where all I see is darkness. The only other way out of all this pain right now for me is to die. That's how much this hurts.

Sincerely, Suicidal Thoughts

Dear Suicidal Thoughts,

First, I want to thank you for contacting me. You are so beautiful, and you are so important to the people in your life that you haven't even met yet. You are twenty-three years old. You have a lot of life to live, to experience and to grow. I do know what it feels like to have your heart broken by someone that you loved so much. It happened to me. I didn't want to live either, and I thought killing myself was the only solution. But a complete stranger told me that I was worth living life for ME. She reminded me that I needed ME. She reminded me that there was purpose inside of me that the world needed, although I didn't feel that way about myself. I thought that I was useless and that if my own mother rejected me, what purpose did I have? Now, here I am today writing you this letter because I realized, even more at this moment, that my purpose was to be here to remind you like I was reminded. You are WORTH LIFE. YOU ARE WORTH LIVING. YOU ARE WORTH HAVING all the good things that you will encounter in your life as you mature in age. I wouldn't be honest with you if I didn't tell you that you will have other challenges. You may have several other heartbreaks, or you may break some hearts yourself. You will go through other ups and downs, and you may fail in some areas. But that's what life consists of. We have to experience things, such as heartbreaks, to help us become and learn who we are in our journey. This is just a part of life's journey. One day, you will get married and become a mother, and then you will be able to do for your children what your mother failed to do for you. I know I don't know you personally, but I care about you. I want you to LIVE. I want you to experience everything that life has on the list for you to accomplish. I know that I am incapable of repairing your heart and only time will mend you, but you will heal, and you are going to meet other young gentlemen, and you're going to be so happy that you did. No one on this earth is worth you taking your life. I want to provide you with a number to call for help. You

127

don't have to repeat the suicide cycle in your father's family. You can break this cycle. It can end with you! Today, right now! You are not a mistake, and you are not crazy. I need you to call this number as soon as you read this letter, and I need you to write me back. I want to hear back from you. Please call the number. I know there is someone that will be able to help get you in a better state of mind. I am not a professional in this area. I just give the best advice that I can give to all the letters I receive. But I don't have to be an expert to know that YOU ARE WORTH LIFE!!! The earth needs you. Again, please reach back to me to let me know if you reached out to anyone. If you need to write me every day, write me every day. I will do whatever it takes to keep you here, so you can complete your purpose in your life. I will be looking to hear back from you. Stay Strong!

Sincerely, Gurlé

National Suicide Prevention Lifeline: This line provides confidential aid for people in crisis, for loved ones, and for professionals. Call this number 1-800-273-8255, and visit this site for more information, https://suicidepreventionlifeline.org.

The National Alliance on Mental Health: This 24-hour helpline, 1-800-950-6264, provides aid and counseling for people experiencing a mental illness and for the family and friends of people with a mental illness. People can also text "NAMI" to 741741 for free and private crisis counseling.

Dear Gurlé,

I wrote you two weeks ago regarding my *Suicidal Thoughts.* I just want to thank you for providing me with the guidance that I needed. I reached out for help, and I am on my way to recovery. I won't say that the thought doesn't still cross my mind, but it's not as bad as it was before. It all came out one night, one week ago, when I told my mother that I hated her. I admitted to her there were many times I nearly blew my brains out with a gun, but each time before I could pull the trigger, I was interrupted by her or my sister. My mother looked at me as tears fell from her eyes. She told me this was her biggest fear, and this is why she and my father separated. I learned through my mother that my father's side of the family suffers with mental health issues. After being evaluated by the doctors, it was confirmed that I developed the trait from my father's family. I am currently getting the help that I need. I am on medication and being closely monitored by my doctors right now. I have been in the hospital since last week. I may be released in the next two weeks or so. I just want to thank you for stalling me. After I wrote you, I waited for your response letter in the mail every day. That helped keep me from pulling the trigger. I was crying out for help. And you helped me in more ways than you know. Please continue giving advice to anyone who reaches out to you. There are so many other young adults and older adults who are suffering with suicidal ideations. I would have never known that mental health issues ran in my family. I am positive that there are a lot of other people who have mental health issues, but it's going unnoticed every day. I am focusing on me right now and getting my mind at a steady and positive place. My ex-boyfriend came to visit me at the hospital. He apologized for the way he ended things with us. We decided to remain friends after all. I also apologized for slashing his tires and all the bad things that I did when he broke up with me. My mother has been at the hospital every day. She's beginning to show that she cares about me. I have a long road ahead of me, and I'm taking one step at a time. I'm also receiving grief counseling through the hospital to help me with my father's death. I discovered throughout all of this that I blocked that part out of my life and out of my mind. The pain was still there, and I never sought any help after learning that my father jumped off of a bridge and took his life. My mother never brought it up after his funeral, and we carried on with our lives as if it never happened. Now everything is coming to the surface. The counseling sessions are something that I definitely need. Hopefully, my mother will seek help one day, too. As for me, I AM WORTH LIFE! Therefore, I WILL FIGHT FOR MY LIFE! Thank you.

Sincerely, Suicidal Thoughts

Dear Suicidal Thoughts,

This letter brought tears of joy to my eyes. I am so happy to hear that you are still here, living, breathing and going through life. I am also happy to hear that you are getting the help that you need. Please stay in contact with me as long as you need to. I am glad that I was able to assist you in any way. And yes,

YOU ARE WORTH LIFE!!

Please take care of yourself and remember that I am only one letter away.

Sincerely, Gurlé

You're now preparing to Fly…

Dear Gurlé,

I have a *Broken Relationship with my Mother,* and it's been this way most of my life. I grew up in a single-family home with my mother and two brothers. I don't have the same father as my brothers, but they share the same father. I am the middle child. I remember my mother being in an on-and-off relationship with my brothers' father for years. My oldest brother is two years older than me. My youngest brother is two years younger than me. My parents met during their early childhood. They grew up together in the same neighborhood. They reconnected with each other after my mother ended her relationship with my brother's father. My father was a handsome man. I remember all the ladies ogling over him. He was a lady's man. I learned from my mother's sister that my father was my mother's first true love and her first heartbreak. My father cheated on my mother when they were in high school, and they went their separate ways. When they reunited, I was conceived. My mother and father didn't stay together long after I was born. When I was a year old, my mother reconnected with my brother's father again. I didn't see much of my father growing up. However, my brothers' father was always in and out of our home. I never felt connected to him, and I often felt a disconnection from my mother. When I turned nine, I really took notice of the difference in the way my mother treated me over the way she treated my brothers. She was much stricter with me. My mother never hugged me or told me that she loved me during those years. My mother was so mean towards me. My brothers got away with murder. They could never do any wrong in my mother's eyes. If I had money for candy, she made me share with my brothers, but she didn't enforce the same rules on them like she had always done with me. By the time I was thirteen, I really hated my mother. I used to pray every night to God that she would die the next morning. But she would never die. I didn't like how she spoke to me, especially when she called me names if I did something that she didn't like. She called me stupid and dumb, and I believed her at times. My mother never told me that I was pretty or that I was important, but she boasted over my brothers daily. I developed a very close relationship with my paternal great aunt. She treated me so nicely, and she always said positive things to me. She even admitted to me one day that my mother didn't treat me right. I overheard her telling my mother once, too, that how she treated me was wrong. My mother took it out on me, and she didn't allow me to have any other visits with my great aunt, but that didn't stop me from calling her. My mother seemed to love not only my brothers, but her friend's children, too, but never me. As I got into my teen years, I was so focused on getting out of my mother's house. I could not wait until I turned eighteen. I was going to leave and never talk to her again. Well, I did turn eighteen, and I have kept my promise. Today, I am thirty-three years old, and our relationship remains broken. I have two children, and I am happily married. My mother has never met my children or my husband. I have a very close relationship with my two brothers. They are very active in our lives. My brothers finally admitted to me after all these years that I wasn't treated fairly by our mother when we were growing up. And now they are pressuring me to reach out to her despite all of the past hurt and pain she caused. I just feel that I shouldn't be the one trying to repair this damage. I was a child. I did nothing to deserve mistreatment from my mother. My mother had a sister who used to mistreat me as well; the sun raised and shined around her daughters. My mother always took her sister's side over me. This is why I don't communicate with my mother's sister. My aunt played a part, because she never spoke up for me or told my mother that she was wrong for how she mistreated me. They've always blamed me. They made me feel responsible for building a relationship with my mother even as a child. People don't know what went on behind closed doors. I've seen a lot, but I would never reveal what I saw to anyone. No one knows the hurt and rejection that I've encountered all of my life. I love my brothers, and I respect their opinions, but why should I reach out to my mother? Do you think I am wrong for feeling this way? I am an adult now, and I don't have to invite any negativity into my life. My brothers said that my mother is hurt that she never met her grandchildren. Well, I am hurt because of the way that she treated me most of my life. I don't want my children to go through what I've been through with her. Do you feel that my brothers are right? Do you think that I should reach out to my mother? I am beginning to have mixed feelings about this decision. My husband told me to go with my heart. He told me whatever I decided to do he is with me no matter what. What should I do? Please help.

Sincerely, Broken Relationship with my Mother

Dear Broken Relationship with my Mother,

Thank you for your letter and for being so open about your relationship with your mother. This is a very hard topic to discuss because it's also very sensitive. We are taught that we are to always honor our mothers and fathers with respect. But in a lot of cases, there are mothers and fathers who are not honoring their children. There are parents that don't treat their children right and parents that favor one child over the other. This is when the competition begins to play a factor in the homes with children because the children recognize when the parent favors one child over the other. This is how unhealthy competitiveness; sibling rivalry and broken relationships formulate. We are supposed to honor our parents, but it is also written that parents should not provoke their children to anger. I believe that parents should receive the highest level of respect. But I also believe that sometimes you have to separate yourselves from your parents, too, especially if it's causing mental and emotional suffering to your wellbeing. I know a lot of women who don't have relationships with their mothers, and they are damaged because of it. I would never tell you not to talk to your mother, and you cannot concern yourself with anyone's opinions regarding your broken relationship with your mother. Do not allow anyone to persuade you to do something that your heart is not ready to do and your mind is not ready to handle. You went through a lot of rejection. That is the one thing that affects most of the world's population, REJECTION. No one wants to feel unloved or unwanted by friends, spouses, children or their parents. People fall into depression due to feeling rejected. We are created to receive and to give love to those that are placed in our lives. YOU have to decide when you're ready to talk with your mother. You also have to be prepared that your mother may never admit to treating you the way that you interpreted her treatment towards you. She may believe that she gave you the best life. Your mother may never apologize to you or acknowledge

YOUR HURT, and you have to be okay with it. There are a lot of parents who NEED to say I'm sorry to their adult children so they can heal. But that is not always the case. There are a lot of unhealthy friendships and relationships because a hurt little boy or girl grew into a broken adult who carried their emotional, physical or verbal abuse and scars from their childhood. Again, I will never tell you not to make things right with your mother. But if you decide to reconnect with your mother, it has to benefit you. It cannot benefit your brothers, mother or your children. It has to benefit your dire need for healing, restoration and fulfillment. At some point in every person's lives, people will have to face the things that caused them the most hurt, which is called healing, growth and FORGIVENESS. You seem to have a great support system from your husband and brothers. Take your time, and allow your heart to guide you, to make the right decision for YOU at this moment where you currently are in your life. I wish you the best, and I would love to hear back from you once you've made a decision.

Sincerely, Gurlé

Dear Gurlé,

I wrote you about my *Broken Relationship with my Mother* last month. I want to thank you for taking the time to write me back. I've decided to give myself some more time before reaching out to my mother. I do plan to reach out to her one day soon, but not now. I am in a place where I am still healing and learning to love myself. I'm a little sensitive in some areas, but I've come a long way. I don't want to move backwards. When I go before my mother, I don't want to go in anger, hurt or pain. I want to be in a better place mentally where I can receive whatever it is, she has to say to me in return. As you stated, she may not feel that she did anything wrong to me, and I need to be able to handle it. God is working on me now. I have two children, and I could never imagine my life without them, so it's still very hurtful to me that I didn't receive the love from my mother that I give my children. I'm human, and I understand that tomorrow isn't promised to anyone. I know that time is valuable, but I have to go in front of my mother mentally prepared for me. I know that in due time everything will work out, and whatever comes from our talk, whether we restore our relationship or not, I want to be at a place where I AM OKAY with the end result. I don't want to bring any more baggage to my marriage due to any of this. My brothers understand my decision, and my husband is on my side no matter my decision. As far as my mother physically meeting my children, I'm not ready for that to happen. However, my children know of their grandmother. I have showed them pictures, and I've talked about her to them. My children are three and five years old, so I have time. I did send a picture of my children through my brothers to give to my mother, so that is a start, right? Again, thank you so much for your time and your advice. I'm going to take each day at a time.

Sincerely, Broken Relationship with my Mother

"Parents need to apologize when they've hurt their children, so their children can heal and won't grow into broken adults."
– Caprice Lamor –

Dear Gurlé,

I am what people consider to be a *Pretty Girl*. I was never the ugly duckly growing up. I never had any issues with dating. I was always the most sought out girl by the guys in my highschool, college and amongst my girlfrirends. Although I am called the "Pretty Girl," I have never felt that way about myself. I'm often prejudged by people daily based on my appearance. People automatically assume that I am conceited, over confident and probably over the top. Not because I've demonstrated these behaviors towards anyone. They just assume these things about me because of my appearance. When I attended highschool, I used to get into physical and verbal altercations all the time with girls. They didn't like me due to how I looked or because a boy that they liked, liked me. On my job, it's even worse. I'm disliked at work because of the way that I look. My supervisor hates me and it's no secret. She makes my job complicated because she is intimidated by me. I almost quit my job twice because of the way that she constantly harasses me and picks at everything that I do. My other coworkers have also noticed how she mistreats me, too. Grown women are the worst haters. They get angry with me because their husband, or whomever he is to them, looks at me. I don't want him. People have no clue that I don't even like myself most days, yet alone feel pretty. I've never seen myself the way others see me, and I probably never will. I remember when I was eleven years old, I told my mother that I wanted to become a model, and she told me that I wasn't pretty enough to be a model. My friends assume that my life is so good just because of the way that I look, but they have no idea how I suffer with low self-esteem issues and even depression. I down myself around other women just so they won't feel intimated by me. I don't ever look at myself in the mirror, especially when I'm in the restroom filled with other ladies admiring themselves. I guess it's because

I don't want them to feel that I think I'm better than them. It's the worst feeling in the world to be disliked by the people you know, and don't know, just because of the way that you look. I don't go out much, and I stay to myself all the time. The last time I went out with some friends it was a horrible night. That night we went to a Super Bowl party, and one of my girlfriends confessed to having a crush since the ninth grade on a guy we saw from our high school. She was hoping to catch his attention. But guess who he was more interested in getting to know. Yes, me. He confessed to having a crush on me since high school, and he wanted to know if we could go out. Of course, I declined and I told him that I wasn't interested. I would never do that to my friend. He paid her no mind the entire night, no matter how hard she tried to get his attention. He told me in front of her that he wasn't giving up on me until I accepted a date with him. The guy never knew that my friend was interested in him. I also never told him because I didn't want to make things awkward for her. Since that night, my girlfriend has cut all communication with me because of what happened. I had no control over what occurred. I turned the guy down in front of her each time. I showed him no interest at all, and I did everything to make her feel comfortable about the situation. She pretended she was cool and that he was her past crush. But I would have never broken the friendship code. I haven't spoken to her in five months. I called her, and she blocked my number. She also unfriended me on all her social media sites. The strange part is I saw the same guy a week ago, and he told me again that he was interested in dating me. But I turned him down. I told him all about my friend and that she was really interested in him. He told me that she wasn't his type and that she also wasn't my friend. He told me that night at the Super Bowl party, she kicked my back in to anyone that would listen. I wasn't surprised. He told me that I was everything that he desired and to consider giving him a chance. He gave me his number and told me to think about it. I'm going to be completely honest with

142

you, he is a really nice guy. He has so much good going for him. He is also very attractive. I've always had a secret crush on him as well. But I will never tell him or anyone else that, especially after learning that my friend liked him, too. I would have never done that to her, but now that I know how she kicked my back in, I'm considering giving him a shot. I don't know what to do. It's crazy how we live in a world where people judge you on your appearance and not your heart. I don't want to continue living the rest of my life being disliked, because of the way that I look, which causes other women to feel insecure about themselves. I hope my letter doesn't come off to you as vain. But you'd be surprised how many people on this earth are disliked for no other reason besides the way that they look. This has been my entire life. And yes, it makes me insecure because I want to be liked and accepted by my peers. What am I supposed to do if my appearance is the first thing that people notice when they meet me? I am glad that I am looked at as a Pretty Girl. But I am more saddened that I am looked at as a threat because I am a Pretty Girl. I've lost several friendships and even relationships because of others' insecurities towards me. How do I learn to embrace my beauty in a humble and positive way, without feeling insecure about myself? How do I embrace my beauty without being apologetic because of who I am, not just on the outside, but on the inside, too. What woman doesn't want to be looked to as being pretty? And there is not one woman on this earth who wants to be disliked because she is pretty either. I understand that beauty is in the eyes of the beholder, but can you please help me to find myself in this?

Sincerely, Pretty Girl

Dear Pretty Girl,

Thank you for being so transparent and no, your letter doesn't come off as vain. What's happening to you happens to many women everyday. We live in a world where you are judged because of how you look, dress, or even what you have financially. But one thing you must understand is that you cannot help the way that God created you to be. Everything that God creates is beautiful, and if the people who come in contact with you don't feel the beauty of God in them, that's not your fault. You should never have to walk around demoting who you are to help build others up. Embrace yourself with humility and great character. Those who come in contact with you, those who serve your purpose, will learn you from the inside out. I am sorry to hear that your friend ended her friendship with you because a guy liked you over her. You displayed your loyalty as her friend by turning the young man down. But if it were the other way around, would she have considered your feelings? You have to embrace your beauty regardless of what anyone thinks about you. No matter what ever happens, don't you ever dim your light for anyone. They have to deal with their own insecurities. You cannot control a guy's attraction for you. Men are attracted to what they like. If I were you, I would give the guy a chance. I would call him and agree to a date. That person whose feelings you are taking into account was never your friend. I believe you've always known this to be true about her deep down inside. We all have experienced an unauthentic friendship once or twice in our lives. It's time for you to stop feeling ashamed about who you are and embrace your beauty on the outside, but most importantly on the inside. If you are never liked by anyone else on this earth, even family, just know that God loves you. He is the one that created you. He made you, and you are beautiful in his eyes. Go and hug yourself and thank God for those GOOD GENES!! It's okay to know you got it. But just always remain humble along the way. I wish you the best.

Sincerely, Gurle

Dear Gurlé,

I am going through a terrible *Divorce.* I've been married to my husband for 5 ½ years. I knew before saying "I do" that he wasn't the one for me, but I desperately wanted to be married because I had a point to prove to those who spoke against our relationship. To be quite honest, he wasn't even my type. I wasn't physically attracted to him at first. I was attracted to his work ethics and the relationship he had with his family. He appeared to be a nice, sweet gentleman. He opened and closed the doors for the ladies, and due to his mannerism and personality, a lot of the ladies had their eyes on him. But behind closed doors, I learned that he was a totally different person. He was a liar, a cheater, and he did a lot of other things that I am too embarrassed to share. We never had children together, which is a good thing. I did fall in love with him, and I grew more attracted to him each day. Everyone who learned that I was his wife couldn't believe it. They have asked him in front of me, *"How did you get her?"* He was proud to call me his wife. I was like a trophy to him. I wasn't the average wife; I cooked, cleaned and I knew my place. We both had great careers, so money was never an issue at all. Our problems all started when he first cheated. We weren't even married one full year. I was devastated and I shut down. By the second year, I had mentally left our marriage, but I still loved him. After that, I also found out from one of his closest friends that he slept with one of my friends. I was so hurt. His own friend told me that my husband didn't deserve to have me, and that he deserved to be with a woman like me, not my husband. His friend told me that I was beautiful, and he's always imagined that I was his wife. And in the heat of the moment, tears, anger and hurt, I slept with his friend. I wanted my husband to feel the hurt and betrayal that he put me through and all of the mental and emotional abuse that I had suffered being married to him. I know that I was wrong; two wrongs don't make a right. My husband found out what happened between his friend and I, because I told him the truth. He was so upset after I told him that he began breaking everything in the house. He then asked me, "*How could you disrespect me in that way?*" And I said to him, "*Dude, really? After all the times you've disrespected me by sleeping with other women? Now your ass knows how it feels to be betrayed. I don't regret any of my actions.*" We continued to argue for several minutes. Then he left the house slamming all the doors. I don't know if he ever confronted his friend or not, but I never saw or heard about his friend again. We are currently in the process of completing the divorce paperwork. But now he doesn't want to sign the divorce papers. It's been nine months since the incident occurred. I have been staying with a friend while he remains in our townhouse. He's been sending me flowers once a week to my friend's apartment. He's even written me a two-page letter stating he is sorry for the way that he's treated me and he has also forgiven me for sleeping with his friend. He also asked me to consider marriage counseling before we sign the final divorce documents. I do love my husband, and part of me wants everything to work out, and the other part of me still has some doubts. He has done this in the past before, such as giving me flowers as an apology. But he has never stated that he wanted us to get counseling. He was always against counseling when I recommended it. He believed that all counselors did is take your money. We will be married six years next month. I am thirty-six years old, and I don't want to start over again, but I don't want to be in a marriage if I'm not happy. At this moment, with everything that my husband has taken me through, I still love him, and I am in love with him. What I did with his friend was unacceptable. I had no excuse. Despite all the women he cheated on me with and despite cheating on me with my friend, I still was wrong. The average woman would call me crazy for considering saving my marriage because of his long history of cheating. But I love my husband, I do. He asked me to let him know by the end of the week if counseling is something that I'm willing to do. He told me that he loved me, and he didn't want to lose me. He told me that he was ready to become the husband that he needs to be for me. My girlfriend told me I would be a fool if I took him back. Yet her boyfriend, not her husband, cheated on her and made two babies while in their eight-year relationship together. Yes, eight years and yes, they are still together. It baffled me because this is my husband, why shouldn't I give him another chance? Meanwhile, she's given her boyfriend several chances. I must admit that I am afraid. I don't want to agree to work things out with my husband and then he reverts back into his old ways. What should I do? Should I give my husband another chance? Or should I just go through with our divorce?

Sincerely, Divorce

Dear Divorce,

Wow. Thank you for sharing. I'm going to get right to the point with you. If you love your husband and you want to save your marriage, and both of you are on the same accord with this decision, SAVE YOUR MARRIAGE!! I never understood why individuals run away from counselors, therapists, and psychologists. We all need some extra help every now and then. There are so many marriages that could have been saved that failed in divorce. No one will EVER have the perfect marriage. All marriages will go through their ups and downs. It's different if a person or persons are not willing to fix, solve, rebuild and restore their marriages. Then divorce would be their only option IF they are not willing to make it work. If one person is willing to make it work but the other partner is not willing, most likely divorce will be the only result. In your situation, you and your husband both made mistakes. He's cheated on you several times, and you've cheated just once. It still doesn't make it right. You both were wrong in this marriage. Even if you've never cheated and you both were willing to make it work, I would still tell you to SAVE YOUR MARRIAGE. It's easy to divorce; it's much harder to work it out because so many people are against marriages today. Marriage is not looked at in the same perspective as it was looked at years ago. The divorce rates were never this high, and during those times, marriages were looked at in a respectful way. Few respects the covenant of marriage. You have to guard and respect your own covenant. Also, I would never take advice from a single woman who has never been married and believes a *Common Law Marriage* is a real marriage. Most women are single because their "what they refuse to do or take" list is sometimes unrealistic. When you are in a marriage, it's not as easy to walk away like you could in a dating relationship. If you want your marriage, you should call your husband and get the counseling that you guys need to begin the healing process of your marriage. You cannot be concerned about other people's opinions concerning your marriage. And you should never discuss your husband with your female friends, good or bad. It's okay to seek wise counsel from married women who have been married for years. You could learn a lot from them. But your household should always be private. People don't need to know your bedroom business. If you do decide to stay married, you have to let the past go and don't you ever make the mistake of sleeping with another one of your husband's friends. No matter what he does. The best response if you remain unhappy is to leave. Thank you for reaching out. I wish you both a newfound love in your marriage and all new beginnings.

Sincerely, Gurlé

Dear Gurlé,

We didn't go through with the *Divorce*. We decided to seek counseling after all. It wasn't an easy process, trust me. But I've learned something that humbled me during this process. I learned that I wasn't perfect after all in my marriage, and I blamed my husband for a lot of things. The counseling sessions became healing, therapeutic sessions for me. I didn't realize that I was scarred from my past relationships and my broken relationship with my father. I held my husband's infidelity over him for years, and even though I told him that I forgave him, I always threw his infidelity back in his face. I didn't help the situation, and although he was wrong for cheating on me, I had to take some ownership as well. My husband disclosed during one of our sessions how I often made him feel less than a man. He disclosed what he was exposed to as a child. His mother was a promiscuous woman. He saw his mother having affairs with other men while married to his father. The weight of him having to hold this secret as a child was too much for him to bear. He felt bad because his father was a good parent, husband and provider. He felt his father didn't deserve to be treated that way. Both of his parents are now deceased. I've never heard him talk much about them until now. It was always a very touchy topic, so I would never ask him too many questions about his folks. I also blamed my husband for things that he had nothing to do with in my life. I didn't realize that I was doing it. I am so happy that I contacted you because sometimes we look at what the other person did to us, but we fail to see our own faults. Again, I am not justifying my husband's infidelity; I'm just acknowledging that I was just as wrong in some parts of our marriage as well. I know it's been one year since your response letter. I just felt compelled to write you back. My husband did a complete 180 change. Don't get me wrong, his past tries to creep up from time to time. I'm referring to those women who believe that they can still have him if they want him. Oh yes, there are some women out here that are worse than men. Before he changed his phone number, they would call and text him half naked pictures trying to convince him to be with them. Now these women I'm referring to know that my husband is married, and some of them are married women, too. After we got back together, there were a couple of women who alleged that my husband had fathered their children. It was a lot to deal with, but it wasn't too farfetched from the possible truth. My husband had been with a lot of women, and he could have easily conceived a child during his infidelity. But I am happy to say that out of the two women who were sure he was the father to their children; the paternity tests were both negative. My husband no longer hides his cell phone, and I have his passwords to everything. There are no more secrets in our marriage. At least I'm hoping that's the case. I feel like we're in a new marriage. We've fallen in love for the first real time. We are experiencing a different love with one another. I am also happy to announce that I am seven months pregnant with our first baby girl. We have placed God in the front of our marriage, and we pray together as a family. My husband has become the husband that I've always wanted, but most importantly needed. I have also stepped up to the plate as a wife. I am more understanding and less sensitive. I no longer bring up his past whenever we have a disagreement. We do still have our disagreements every now and then, but our disagreements are much healthier. It's normal to disagree. Marriage will never be perfect for anyone. I've also learned to keep friends out of my business. I don't need to share everything. Thank you again for not being judgmental despite knowing both of our wrongs. You were a big encouragement to me and the one reason why I decided to give my husband another chance. I appreciate your honesty and realness. Keep doing what you do. There are a lot of girls out there like me who could use sound and wise advice from someone like you.

Sincerely, Divorce

Dear Divorce,

Thank you for reaching back out to me. It's been a long time since we've last written each other. Congratulations with your new bundle of joy and your newfound love in your marriage. What you stated in your letter to me was very profound. Most women are hurting in their relationships and marriages over the wounds someone else left on their hearts. I was married before, and I blamed my husband for every wound caused on my heart after he first cheated on me. I no longer saw him. I only saw the infidelity, and I reminded him what he did to me during every argument, big or minor. I hated him, and I was very angry at him. I blamed the divorce and all of our marital issues on him. It wasn't until two years after we were divorced that I realized that I had a lot of identity issues within my marriage with him. It hit me that everything was not completely his fault. I realized that I was a damaged little girl inside of a grown woman's body. I wasn't ready for marriage, no more than him. I carried my expectations and fantasies into what I thought our marriage should be. I expected him to be to me what I lacked from my father, my mother and every other relationship or disappointment from my past. Unfortunately, there are a lot of women who think like I first thought, that because I had my college degree, the great career, that because I could cook and clean and I looked good that I was ready for marriage. You have to be ready mentally, as well. I know now that marriage is made up of so many components. When a person can take accountability for the baggage they carry into their new relationships from their past heartbreak or childhood etc., only then can they be real with themselves. A person with major trust issues didn't just enter into a new relationship and find trust issues there. They came from someplace else. I've learned that it takes two to the make the thing go right or left. I applaud you for identifying your issues and taking accountability for what you didn't do as well. Although we all recognize that your

152

husband was disloyal and unfaithful, it's good to acknowledge that everyone has to take responsibility for the damage that was caused. If more people could admit they're wrong, even when they are more right in a matter, this world would be a better and happier place. Thank you for allowing me to be transparent in this letter and for trusting my advice. I am happy to know that you are growing, not just inside your belly, but in maturity as well. Stay happy, stay growing and most importantly, keep God first in your marriage and everyone else out of your personal business. Take care.

Sincerely, Gurlé

Dear Gurlé,

I am in a biracial relationship with a guy and we are truly in love, but his parents are *Racist* towards me because of the color of my skin. My parents are also a biracial married couple. They have been married for twenty-nine years. My mother's family disowned her after she became pregnant with me. I am my parents only child. My mother hasn't seen nor spoken with her parents or siblings since she married my father. I am twenty-seven years old. My father is a doctor, and my mother doesn't work. My mother overcame cancer two years ago. Prior to her beating cancer, she worked as a nurse. My mother spends all of her time building foundations to help find the cure for cancer. I met my boyfriend during my freshmen year in college. He had the most gorgeous eyes that I've ever seen. We shared two classes together. I instantly had a crush on him, but I never showed any signs. I didn't look like him. I knew that eventually it would become an issue because we came from two totally different backgrounds. I also remembered what my parents went through. As we approached the end of our freshmen year in college, my friend, who is also his sister's best friend, invited me to her pool party. His sister was a junior in college, but her best friend was a sophomore. They've been best friends since elementary school. I went to her pool party that night, and he was there. I was sitting alone at the pool when he came over to me and playfully splashed water towards me, which ignited a playful water fight between us two. During our water fight he picked me up and threw me into the pool. I felt at that moment there was a connection between us. That night we sat near the pool and talked for hours straight. We just ignored the party and everyone around us. As it began to get late, everyone began leaving the party. He walked me to my car, and he told me that he really enjoyed talking to me. We just stood there looking at each other. No one was around. It was just the two of us. I told him that I had a good time, too. I had butterflies moving around my stomach, and I couldn't control that warm feeling inside of me. I opened my car door to get inside, and when I turned back around to tell him goodnight, he kissed me. After we kissed, I just stood there mesmerized and in disbelief. We said goodnight, and I got into my car and drove away. It was a while before we spoke again after that night. The summer was coming to an end when I received a phone call from him. He told me that he had been trying to find me since that night. He said that he managed to get my number discreetly. I told him that I went back home with my parents for the summer break and had immediately left after the semester ended. He told me that he couldn't stop thinking about me since that night. He told me that he really wanted to spend some time with me alone before the fall semester began. I was feeling those butterflies in my stomach once again. We agreed to meet up with each other. I drove back to school one week early so I could see him. And when I did, the feelings were still there. His eyes were my weakness. He told me that he couldn't stop thinking about me since that night and that he wanted to know if we could become more than just friends. I agreed to get to know him better. We both understood that our relationship may not be accepted by everyone even in today's time because we come from different races and backgrounds. He openly told me that his parents didn't agree with dating outside of your race. He admitted that his parents were racist towards certain people and cultures, but he told me that he didn't agree with what his parents believed. He said that people should be free to love who they choose to love. We were living a secret life. My parents are aware of our relationship, but his parents are not. We were about to graduate from college in a few days, and we wanted to spend the rest of our lives together. He agreed to finally tell his parents about us. He was certain that his parents would disown him once they found out. I love him, but I didn't want to cause division between him and his family. But at the same time, I was tired of hiding us. We both loved each other, and we wanted to get married. He told me no matter what happened he will choose us. Well, we graduated college. He told his family about me, and they made him choose. But he didn't choose me. I am devastated and hurt. I know that he still loves me. It's been one year and eight months since we've spoken. I found out from his sister's best friend that he is seeing someone else whom his parents approve of, of course. But I know he isn't happy with her. They are engaged to be married in two months. My mother told me that it's time for me to move on. She said that we live in a world where some people will never accept biracial relationships. But I can't let him go. How am I supposed to move forward, as if three years didn't exist between us? He just walked away like that. He went to tell his parents about me, and he never came back. It hurts. I watched my parents go through so much just to be together. I never thought that this would be me. How do you move on from someone that you know loves you? We spent the last three years together. He told me that he was in love with me, and that he had never loved another woman the way that he loved me. What should I do? Should I just pretend what we had never existed or should I fight for us? I'm hurt, confused and broken.

Sincerely, Dealing with Racism

Dear Dealing with Racism,

I am so sorry to hear what you've been through. One thing for certain is that we cannot turn our love on and off like a light switch. It takes time to heal, and it takes time to move on. The world that we live in is the true reality of life. Love should conquer all, but as you learned from your parents, they had to lose their families in order for love to conquer. I know that you are hurting right now, and it's been nearly two years since he made his decision. But eventually you will have to move forward in your life. You have your entire life ahead of you. I don't doubt that he loved you, but he made his choice and he didn't choose you. You have to accept it for what it is, and this may sound harsh, but it's your true reality right now. Whether he goes through with his marriage or not, you have to live your life. In a far away fairytale land, it's every girl's dream on this earth for a guy to be her knight in shining armor. To come and sweep her off her feet and confess his dying love for her. But that may never be every girl's true reality. If you feel that his love is worth fighting for, then you do what you have to do for your heart. But keep in mind that he didn't fight to keep you in his life. If he would have truly fought for you, then his parents would have had no other choice but to accept you. You may never know the reasons why he chose to let you go, and no, it doesn't mean that he didn't love you. He may have considered that he didn't want you to have to live a life of judgement just to be with him. And it could have been too much for him to handle. However, whatever you decide, whether you choose to fight for your love, or choose to move forward, make the right decision for your heart, not your emotions. Life has a sarcastic way of doing things. You just never know who may cross your path. You may end up meeting someone better, and you'll be happy that things didn't work out for you and him. God also has his way of protecting us. I hope that everything works out for you and that you make the best decisions for your heart. One thing

I will tell you is that LOVE has no color. It's okay to love other people who do not look like you or don't share the same race, background and culture as you do. Do not let this discourage you in the future. Thank you for sharing your story. I wish you the best.

Sincerely, Gurlé

Dear Gurlé,

I lost my mother from cancer the day before Christmas six years ago. I was thirty-three years old. Since the passing of my mother I have never felt so *Lonely*. Although I am married with beautiful twin daughters, there is a piece in my heart that is still missing. My mother was my best friend. I could talk to her about anything. We did everything together, and we used to spend countless hours on the telephone talking every other day. As I write this letter to you, tears are coming down my face. The holidays are approaching, and its always been the most difficult time of the year for me. My daughters are five years old, and they love the Christmas holiday, but since my mother passed away, its been hard for me to get into the holiday spirit, especially the way that I should with my children. My husband has to do it all for me. He decorates the tree and bakes the cookies for Santa Claus. He enjoys this time of the year with our daughters, while I sleep in bed all day. It's not only Christmas, but Mother's Day, her birthday and my birthday. I have developed anxiety, and I haven't slept more than five hours a night since the day my mother passed away. I know that you may be thinking it's time for me to let go, but it's so hard for me. I miss her so much. My grief has also caused a strain on my marriage. I am more sad than I am happy. I still have my mother's voice message that she left me on my voicemail. Whenever I need to hear her voice, I just listen to it. After she died, I kept everything in her house the exact way that she left it. You would think that after six years I would be at a different place, but I am still stuck. I was so angry at God for so many years for taking my mother away from me. I stopped praying and attending Sunday services. I tried to process it over and over again in my head. Why did he take her? Especially when I needed her much more. No one ever understood me like my mother. She knew when something was wrong with me before I could even say it. When I had my first heartbreak, she told me that he was going to regret losing me one day. My mother always made me feel like I could conquer anything. She was my rock and my strength. I want to be the mother that my mother was to me, for my daughters. I don't want to miss out on the most special moments of their lives because I am still grieving. I want Christmas to be special again, especially for them. I just don't know how to heal my heart. How to let go. When I see other women celebrating their mothers, I just get to a private area alone and cry. My car has become my personal place to cry, shout and scream. It's the only space where I can hide away from my children and husband. I had no one but my mother. She was all that I ever needed. I know that I need to get myself together because I have two daughters and a husband that needs me, too. I do love my husband, and I thank him for being so patient with me for so long. I know that I have to be what he needs me to be for him and for our children. I feel guilty living a happily ever after life knowing that my mother is not here. I guess I am afraid that if I don't keep my mother's memory alive, no one else will. My daughters were one year old when she passed away. Oh how my mother loved her grandchildren. My mother was the one that told me I was pregnant with twin girls. She knew before the doctors could tell me. I talk to my children about their grandmother all the time. I have her picture in their bedroom and throughout our home. My husband still has both of his parents. There are moments that I get angry that his parents are still here, but both my parents are gone. I know I may sound selfish, but I just miss my mom so much. I've never felt so empty and lonely. I don't care what anyone tells you. There's nothing like losing a parent. It's a feeling that cannot be explained. I know that I have to move on soon. But how do I keep my mother's memory alive, while still moving forward in my life? How do I get through the holidays with my husband and children without grieving? How do I let her go, while still holding on to her precious memories?

Sincerely, Lonely

Dear Lonely,

I am sorry for your loss. Losing a parent is one of the hardest things that any person has to go through. And it's just as hard for a mother when she loses her child. There is no amount of words that I can say to you to help you speed up your healing process. Life doesn't give you a specific time, especially when you are grieving. Holidays are a very tough time for millions of people around the world each year. Not every household is celebrating with joy alongside their loved ones. There are people who are mourning and grieving just like you over the loss of a loved one. You just have to find it in you to turn your grieving into happier memories of your mother. You stated that Christmas was a special holiday when your mother was alive. So, continue to make Christmas a special holiday in her honor. Make new memories with your family while remembering the good memories that you shared with your mother. You can do some of the things with your children that you and your mother used to do together. You can keep your mother's memories without mourning her absence. I know that your mother would want you to create your own special memories with your children as well. I also know that your memories of your mother will never fade away because you will forever carry her in your heart. There are also grief counselors that you can talk to. You may want to look up some local support groups and counselors in your area. You have your husband who loves you and his parents who are also now your parents. Embrace and love the family that's around you, that are still here while you can embrace them. It's okay to have those moments to cry when you miss your mother. But they can be tears of good memories and good times. No one can ever tell you how long to grieve over anyone. You have to decide how you display the memories of your mother, only you. The only thing that will help you is time and the new memories that you create while embracing the old memories that you shared with her. I know for sure that time will give you the acceptance and the confidence that you need to move forward. Time may never fully heal all wounds, but time will soothe your wounds and give you the peace that you need in the end. I wish you the best!!

Sincerely, Gurlé

"Time is valuable because it's in those moments that memories are created."
— Caprice Lamor —

Dear Gurlé,

I recently learned that I was *Adopted.* I am twenty-five years old. I was always a happy person. I grew up with both of my parents who have been married for twenty-seven years. My parents are very successful financially and in their careers. I've never wanted for anything. My first vehicle was a BMW. I went to the best schools, and I grew up in the suburban area with children whose parents were also successful in their careers. I have four sisters and three brothers. I am the second oldest girl. My parents mirror the kind of relationship that I want for myself. I've always looked to them as an example of what life and love should be. I had a decent relationship growing up with my siblings. I always considered my youngest sister to be my best friend. We did everything together. I looked at her like a doll baby. She followed me everywhere I went, and I was always protective of her. I still reside with my parents along with four of my other siblings. My oldest brother got married a year ago, and my oldest sister moved to Europe for a year. One day, I was going through the mail at our home, and I found a letter with my name and parents' names on it. I was puzzled. I had no idea what it could have been. I began pondering, wondering if I should open it or wait for them to come home. I figured since my name was on the letter too that I had the right to open it. I couldn't believe what I was reading. This was impossible. It was a letter regarding my birth mother. As I began reading further, I learned that my parents were not my parents. The letter said my biological mother just died. I was confused. I started looking through our family photo albums. I wanted to study my parents' features. *"I looked just like my mother?"* I thought to myself. I began to hyperventilate, *"Was this all a lie? This life? My family, and the person who I thought I was?"* I sat in disbelief as I tried to strategize how I would approach my parents with this information. At that very moment, I felt disconnected

165

from them and the life I thought was mine. Everything that I had ever felt about my parents was slowly disappearing. Who were these people? And why had they kept this from me my entire life. When my parents came home that evening, I didn't utter a word. I couldn't speak. I just sat there staring at them as they talked, the sound of their voices slowly faded away. My mother asked me if I was okay several times. I told her that I wasn't feeling too well. I went to my room, and I tried to make sense of everything. I was unable to function at work, and I wasn't eating. I took pride in my family and where I came from, but now I didn't even know the real me. My life started falling apart right before my eyes. My boyfriend broke up with me, and my best friend and I stopped speaking. I started breaking out all over my face, and I was looking tired and run-down. Every opportunity that I had, I looked through my mother's personal papers in her office. I couldn't find anything pertaining to me being adopted. She did a great job hiding this information all of these years. One day, sometime later, my mother came home early from work, which was unusual for her. She walked into my bedroom holding the letter in her hand. She sat on the edge of my bed as she began to explain that she knew this day would come. She cried. She told me that I was her daughter and that it didn't matter what anyone said. I learned that my birth parents were a biracial couple. My biological father's parents did not approve of my birth mother because she was of a different race. My parents were fifteen years old when I was born. My biological mother was forced to give me up for adoption, although she didn't want to. My mother told me that my birth parents loved me, but they were too young to care for me. My mother explained that she and my father always wanted a big family. My mother was pregnant with a baby girl, and she went into labor one week early. But due to complications during her delivery, she lost the baby at birth. She was devastated. She told me that God had other plans because my birth mother was giving birth to me in the next room on the same day that she lost her baby girl. She had learned about this young girl shortly after losing her daughter, and my birth mother learned that my mom had lost her baby. My birth mother asked my mother to take me after she heard her story, because she knew that I would get the love that I needed. My birth mother never named me. She told my mother to give me my identity. My birth father never acknowledged my birth mother again after I was born, after he was forbidden by his father. My mother told me that one week later she came home from the hospital with me. My mother stated that no one ever knew that I was not her biological daughter, and they all assumed that I was the little girl that she had carried for nine months. My siblings have no idea that I am adopted. My parents never shared it with anyone, and they never planned to tell me anything about it. My mother promised my birth mother that she would keep her informed about me throughout the years. This is why she knew where to reach her and my dad. My birth mother never had any other children. When my mom was done, I didn't know what to say. I just sat there and cried. I couldn't believe that my life story sounded like a real Lifetime movie. Since the day I learned that I was adopted, I have been trying to rediscover myself. How do I recover from this and move on without having resentment or feeling uncertainty? I am having a very difficult time. I am still hurt because I was lied to, but I am also happy that God gave me my parents. Am I wrong for feeling this way? I have a lot of mixed emotions. I don't want to hurt my parent's feelings by wanting to know more about who I am. I just need advice on how to approach this in a sensitive manner, while still providing myself with the answers that I need and without hurting my parents.

Sincerely, Adopted

Dear Adopted,

Your story is extremely one of a kind. Thank you so much for sharing such personal information. I am truly moved by how your story unfolded. I could only imagine growing up all of your life believing one thing and then learning that the world you knew had hidden secrets. You have the right to feel hurt, confused and lost. Those are your feelings. It's also alright to feel curious about your true identity and to have questions that you need answered. But no one can make that decision for you. This is something you have to decide for yourself. Before you learned you were adopted, you said that life was great and that you were happy. Your parents and your life haven't changed. You still have great parents and siblings that love you unconditionally. You just learned additional information about who you are. Your DNA identifies your roots, but it doesn't identify your character or the person you've become. If you really need to know about your biological family, there are ways to obtain that information without involving your parents. This is a very sensitive subject, not just for you, but for your parents as well. You are an adult now. You don't have to tell your parents anything. You should only tell your parents if you are seeking to build relationships with your birth family. That's just a respectful thing to do. But you need to allow yourself some time to think and meditate before making any decisions. You don't want to make a quick response based off of your current emotions. You also have to ask yourself, would knowing your biological relations change the fact that you grew up in love? Would it change what your parents mean to you? Would it change that you have grown into a responsible adult? If you are happy in your life as you know it to be, you don't have to change it. That's your choice. I look at your story, and I see that God had a purpose for you. Family is who loves and accepts you, not who you're biologically related to. God chose your birth parents to create you, but God chose your parents to be your parents. Your birth mother asked your parents to take you because she felt in her heart that they could give you what you needed. Your birth mother never named you because she wanted your parents to give you your identity. That is true love. You are truly blessed. Your story could have been much worse. There is no wrong or right answer to your feelings. You have to decide what is best for you. No matter what you learn about your birth family, it will never change the fact that your birth mother always loved you, and that your parents love you, too. If you need it, below I have provided a resource for adoptee support and counseling. I wish you the best, and I know that you will make the decision best for yourself and everyone involved.

Sincerely, Gurlé

American Adoptions: To find support and resources for adult and child adoptees, call 1-800-236-7846 or visit https://www. americanadoptions.com/adoption/adoptee-support-resources.

"Family is who loves and accepts you, not who you're biologically related to."

-Caprice Lamor-

Dear Gurlé,

I have always been the *Black Sheep of the Family.* It all started from my childhood. I was always considered to be my paternal grandmother's "favorite" grandchild. My father became addicted to drugs, and my grandmother took me in to live with her. My grandmother has two sons and three daughters. I was practically raised with my aunts and uncles. I have an uncle who I am one year older than. I went through a lot in my life. My birth mother has been on drugs since my birth. I haven't seen my mother in over one year. The last time I saw her she was high in the streets. My father is not as bad as my mother. He at least tries to be a part of my life, and he genuinely seeks the help that he needs. Unfortunately, he always relapses and returns back to using drugs. During these periods of time, I usually don't see my father for days or even weeks. I know when he goes absent for a long period of time that he is using again. I appreciate the fact that my father doesn't want me to see him under the influence. I have never seen my father using drugs, and I have never seen any drug paraphernalia in our home. Regarding my mother, however, I have seen it all. One day, I walked in on my mother giving fellatio to a complete stranger for money. The sad part is she didn't stop nor did she feel ashamed that I saw her. When I was thirteen years old, my mother's boyfriend masturbated right in front of me. I told my mother, and she called me a liar. She said that I was just like my father. I've never shared this part of my life with anyone, not even my best friend. I guess I just buried it in the back of my mind. Despite all that I've been through, I have my head on straight. I am a college graduate, and I am currently working on my Master of Arts in Early Childhood Education. I don't drink or smoke, and I have strong faith and belief in God. I attend church every Sunday. My paternal grandmother is Catholic. I had no other choice but to attend church daily and repent for my sins when I was living with her. By attending church, I've developed strong morals and values, and I strive everyday to live my life right. But my journey to get here was much harder than it appears. My grandmother has been the mother to me that I needed during the most vulnerable times of my life. It's unfortunate that my aunts and uncles don't see it that way. I have cousins around my same age whose parents always felt that my grandmother treated me better than their children. It may have appeared that way to them, but they each had their mother and father present in their lives. They went to the best schools, and they've always financially had more than me. My grandmother always tried to make up for the things that I didn't receive from my parents. Growing up without having a relationship with your mother or father can be very hard on a child. My mother once blamed me for her drug addiction, and she's always treated her family better than me. Anything that they say against me she believes them. The sad part is I go through just as much with my father's side of the family, too. My grandmother, the one person who truly loves me and shows her cares and concerns for me, is constantly under attack by her children because of me. Some of my cousins also dislike our grandmother and feel the same way as their parents. I am always compared to my other cousins' successes, and their parents are always boasting and bragging about their children's accomplishments, but when anything goes well in my life, it's not a big deal and it's never acknowledged. I never get invited to any family gatherings or events on either side of the family. I feel like a nobody to my family. Does it hurt? Absolutely. It's one thing to have enemies in the streets and false friends. But when you have family members who don't like you and they really cannot justify why, it's truly sad. I promised myself that I was going to let go of everyone and continue to focus on my life, which I have been doing, but no matter what happens, I always seem to be at the top of the family conversations. The word always gets back to me about things that I really have nothing to do with. Today, I am twenty-nine years old. I don't have any communication with my mother at all. My father has been missing for a few months. We have searched for him in the streets, as well as contacted the morgues and hospitals, but nothing has come up about his whereabouts. I am drained and tired of babysitting my parents. I am tired of being blamed for the reason why my aunts, uncles, and cousins don't have a relationship with my grandmother. I am ready to find love and to start my own family. Am I being selfish right now? I don't get the support from my family that I need, and it's always been just me and my grandmother in my eyes. Because I have a relationship with God, I don't want to appear to be hypocritical. But I am tired of my family and the way that they have always treated me my entire life. They will never admit that they have mistreated me, and I am okay with it. My cousins may never admit that I did nothing wrong to them, and I am okay with that, too. I just want to make sure that I am not being selfish about my feelings, especially regarding my parents, before I move on with my life.

Sincerely, Black Sheep of the Family

Dear Black Sheep of the Family,

Thank you for taking the time to share your story. I must say that you are one strong and courageous young lady. One thing that I have learned about life is that we CANNOT select our family. We CANNOT select our parents. We CANNOT choose whose DNA and blood we get to share. But we CAN choose who to have in our lives, especially as an adult. When we are younger, we have to accept how things are until we are wiser in years and are able to make our own conscious decisions. Despite not having the ability or the power to choose our parents, we have to love and honor our parents no matter what. I know that you've been through a lot as a child growing up with both of your parents. But your parents are who God gave YOU. We must honor and always show respect to our parents. It does not excuse how your parents treated you, and all the pain that you've endured has not went unnoticed. Your parents were wrong. You did not ask to be here. Your parents were two adults that made the decision to have you. You should not feel responsible or be blamed for whatever life decisions they've made in their lives. You are and will ALWAYS be the child. No matter how old in age you become, your parents were always the adults in the situation. They knew better regardless of any addictions that they had. In a perfect world, our parents are supposed to provide, nurture, protect and ensure that their children receive the appropriate healthcare, education and love that their children are supposed to receive. But unfortunately, you have some parents who do not provide these things for their children. There are systems in place such as Child Protective Services, which was created to protect children from some of the things that you've encountered as a child. It's hurtful that parents have to be forced by law to provide just the basic needs for their own children. You were placed in a safe environment with your paternal grandmother, and it should have never been an uncomfortable environment for you. Your grandmother saw that you needed to be rescued, and she reacted the way most grandparents would have reacted. You felt mistreated by your family because they felt that you were favored more by your grandmother. You feel like The Black Sheep of The Family because you feel that you don't belong. They made you feel unwanted, not just your father's family but your mother's family as well. As you stated in your letter to me, Let It Go! You can love your family from a distance, and you can continue to wish them well in life. No, this does not make you a selfish person. Even family can be jealous of you, too. And as for your parents, continue to keep an open door for them. You stated that you attend church and that you have a personal relationship with God. Do not close the door on your parents. This does not mean that you have to babysit them and lose sleep worrying if they are okay. Just continue to pray for your parents. One day, you may get the answers that you need, or you may never get the answers that you need from your parents. But appreciate the fact that you've made it through most things that some people, especially at your age, would have lost their minds over. According to statistics you should be on drugs, promiscuous, uneducated, troubled, dead, and/or homeless in the streets. But YOU MADE IT with two parents that were and still are addicted to drugs. Yes, go and live your life. Go and fulfill all your dreams and desires. But please do me one favor, forgive your parents and forgive your family. You were never "The Black Sheep of The Family." You were the shining light at the end of the dark tunnel. God had his hands on you your entire life. It's a blessing that you were not lost in the system. Your grandmother was placed in your life by God because you serve a purpose!! When you look back over your life, keep in memory how God preserved you through it ALL!!

Sincerely, Gurlé

Guide for Children of Addicted Parents:
americanaddictioncenters.org SAMHSA's
National Hotline 1-800-662-HELP (4357) or TTY: 1-800-487-4889
English | Spanish   samhsa.gov

Dear Gurlé

I am *Unhappily Married and Living a Lie,* but everyone in our lives thinks that we have the best marriage in the world. I met my husband nine years ago at a business conference through a mutual friend. I've known our mutual friend since I was a little girl, so I trusted his judgement. My husband and I became more acquainted as time went by and we began dating. We dated for eight months before we made our relationship status official. Then, after dating for almost two years, he proposed to me, and we got married on the 17th day of August. We immediately began a family, and I became pregnant with our first son, and one year and five months later, I became pregnant with our second son. Life appeared to be looking great. I married the man of my dreams. I had two beautiful children. We had the American dream, the house and the white picket fence. We went to Mass every Sunday, and we prayed together as a family. I loved my husband, and I was very happy in our marriage. We were the married couple that all of our friends and family looked up to. We inspired a lot of couples, especially single men and women; we gave them hope. Everyone strived to have a marriage like ours. After we celebrated our sixth wedding anniversary, things started to shift in our marriage. My husband grew more distant from me. He wasn't calling home to check in with me like he'd done most of our marriage. He was coming home late at hours, and he acted as if he hated me at times. He barely wanted to touch me. One weekend, I missed my husband so much I made arrangements to have our children stay over at their grandparents' home, so I could have some alone time with him. I got my hair done, and I got a bikini wax. I purchased sexy lingerie from the mall, and I cooked a nice dinner. I also had dessert ready, and I made sure there was plenty of whipped cream. I had soft music playing in the background with candles lit all throughout the house. When my husband arrived home, he was caught by surprise. I touched his lip with my finger before he could utter a word. I told him that it was all about him that night. I began taking off his clothes piece by piece. I led him into the bathroom where I had a nice hot bath waiting for him. I washed every part of his body, and I gently dried him off. I guided him to our bedroom as I performed oral sex on him several times throughout the night. He bent me over and pounded me from behind with such hard and rough aggression. I've never seen that side of him, but I loved it. We enjoyed a night of sexual pleasure, food and plenty of dessert. The weekend was going great thus far. We were having so much sex that at one time in the middle of the night while I slept, my husband awoke me with oral sexual pleasure and an orgasm that was out of this world. I was in love all over again with him. I felt that I made the right move and had got my husband back. So, I thought. The following week my husband went back to his same strange behavior towards me. I started questioning if he was cheating on me because what other explanation could it be? I started looking through his phone and computer. I figured out his password when we first got married, just in case I needed to have it. I found nothing. But there was a man that he corresponded with a lot that I've never met. I never even heard him speak about him either. I didn't think anything about it. I felt satisfied to know that it wasn't someone else. But I still couldn't understand what was going on. One night, he came home at three in the morning during a weekday. I hadn't spoken with him that entire day. I was furious, and I'd had enough with walking on eggshells. I asked him what was going on and why was he treating me like his enemy. He told me that he's been going through things at work and he's been feeling overwhelmed and stressed lately. I told him that I was his wife and all he had to do is talk to me. He told me that he needed some time to clear his head and he felt it was best if he left for a few days to be alone. I didn't like the idea of my husband wanting to leave me and our children for a few days, but I was willing to do whatever was needed to help him get back on track. The following day he left to go spend some time alone. He refused to tell me where he would be staying, which I found odd. He told me that he didn't want to be bothered by anyone. He promised to call and check in with me at least once. I didn't have anyone to call to get advice from about what was happening in my marriage. Everyone was always calling us for advice or guidance. The next morning after my husband left, I was moving his briefcase into his office, and a letter fell out. The letter was from the same man whose name I had seen several times in his call history. I sat at his office desk for ten minutes just staring at the letter. I asked myself if I was sure that I wanted to read what was in that letter. I opened the letter, and I began to read. The man kept telling my husband it was time and that he had to the make his move now. I didn't understand what that meant. But he had his address on the letter and the date he wanted my husband to meet him. It was the date that my husband left. I paid our neighbor's teenage daughter to watch our children for a couple of hours. I had to go to the address on the paper. When I pulled up to the home, I saw my husband's vehicle parked on the side of the house. It was gated; therefore, I couldn't see much. I sat there for two hours waiting to see if anyone would come out of the house. I didn't have the guts to go to the gate. As I was about to pull off, a beautiful woman walked out of the home and drove away. I was devastated. *"So that must be her,"* I thought to myself. The babysitter called my phone and said that her parents said she had to get home. I drove back home to get my children because it was getting late. I called my husband's cell ten times, and it kept going to his voicemail. I tried to sleep that night, but I couldn't. I got up and drove our children to their grandparent's house at two in the morning. I then drove back to the same address. When I got there, the gate to the home was open. I parked on the street, and I walked up to the front door of the home. There were big tall beautiful windows. The home appeared to be a five or six bedroom home. The owner had to be rich. I saw a Benz, a BMW and two sports cars parked inside of the four-door garage. As I stood on the front entrance of the home, I was able to look inside the living room. I couldn't believe what I was seeing. My husband was on his knees performing fellatio on another man. As he was giving the man pleasure, my husband looked up towards the window, and he saw me standing there looking at him. He looked as if he'd seen a ghost. My husband quickly jumped up and ran towards the window. He was naked. I couldn't even look at him. He tried to plead with me through the glass. He told me it wasn't what it looked like, but now I understood. I understood why he didn't want me. I ran towards my vehicle crying hysterically. I couldn't grasp what I just saw. I must have driven 90 mph all the way back home. I was so angry. I packed all of his clothes every piece of his shit. I put everything into my vehicle, and then I drove back to the home where he was. This time they were sure to have the gate closed. I threw everything on the ground from my car, his suits, and ties, watches, EVERYTHING, all over the front property before the gate. I caused such a scene that all the neighbors were looking out their windows and peeking through their front doors. I was sure that someone would call the police, but no one did. He wasn't even man enough to come out and face me, his wife and the mother of his two sons. He just left me standing there hurt and crying as I wondered, *"How I will explain this to our children?"* It's been four months since the incident happened. My husband has not been back home, not even to see his sons. I filed for a divorce two weeks after I found him with another man. According to my lawyer, our divorce will be finalized within six months. My husband is not fighting for custody, and he doesn't want visitation with our sons. That broke my heart. He also agreed to give me the house and half of everything without a fight. He wants the marriage to be dissolved immediately. I must admit that I am embarrassed and humiliated. I don't want to show my face to anyone. All of these years we have been living a complete lie. I am going to be the laughingstock of the town. How am I going to explain this to my sons who will grow into men one day? How am I going to explain this to my family and my friends? How can I ever trust another man again? I would rather have learned that he was having an affair with another woman than a man. That makes me feel even worse. The part that hurts the most is that he never apologized. He could at least have told me that it wasn't me, it was him. But he left me to feel rejected, hurt, broken, confused and betrayed. I guess he loves dick much better than he likes pussy! Now I know why he enjoyed hitting me from the back. Most men love all sexual positions. But he always preferred the "doggie style." I am so angry, but I have two sons that need me more than ever. Please help me. I need wise advice on what to do. I am too embarrassed to tell anyone right now. I need more time. I'm not ready for all the questions because there are questions that I still need answers to.

Sincerely, Unhappily Married and Living a Lie

Dear Unhappily Married and Living a Lie,

It is very brave of you to share such personal and intimate information about your marriage. One thing that I know to be true, you are not the only woman that has ever gone through this. And you won't be the last. What I can tell you is give yourself TIME. Time to cry, time to be weak, time to be hurt, time to be angry, time to process everything and time to heal. What you've learned about your husband is not your fault. There is nothing that you could have done any differently in your marriage, sexually or physically, to change his mind about who he is. Please do not let this define who you are as a woman. You are still a mother, daughter, sister and friend to many. You have not changed who you are in your heart. You just gave your heart to a person who lied to you about who they truly were. You have to eventually get to a place of acceptance. You don't have to hide and pretend to the people that you love. You need all the support that you can get right now. I do recommend that you seek counseling or a therapist to help you get clarity and eventually closure. It hurts to learn that your spouse cheated on you, but when you learn it's with the same sex, it's a different kind of hurt. Again, your husband lied to you. He knew that he was living a double life. He's always known that he was gay. I'm just happy that you found out when you did. It could have been much worse. You will get through this. It may take you some time, but you will heal from this. When your sons reach a certain age that you feel is appropriate, you can sit them down and tell them what they need to know about their father. As they mature in age you can disclose a little more to them. But whatever you do, despite everything, give them the opportunity to make their own judgements of their father. You want to keep the door open in case they decide they want a relationship with their father one day. There is no reason to feel embarrassed. You didn't know that your husband was living a lie. You didn't know that your husband preferred men. This is

181

something that he has to deal with, and he will eventually have to face how he treated you and his children. If he never apologizes or if he never takes his part as a father in your son's lives, you have to continue living and moving forward. Please understand that there are millions of men in this world that appreciate women, and they prefer only women. Don't give up hope; there is someone out there for you. Time will give you back trust, and time will give you the answers that you need for you. Stay strong and take time for you. I wish you the best in your future. I know that you are going to get through this, and one day your story will help someone else. Thank you for sharing your story. Always remember that TIME is the key. Take one step at a time, each day at a time. This too shall pass.

Sincerely, Gurlé

Dear Gurlé,

I'm two weeks away from reaching a major *MILESTONE* in my life. I'm turning forty, and I'm having a difficult time coping with it. I'm single, never been married, and I'm without children. I've experienced a one-night stand; I've tried a dating app, and it wasn't for me. I've dated a guy with a criminal record. I've had a Friends with Benefits relationship. I've been cheated on and lied to. I've been the side chick, *when I thought I was the only one.* I've dated a professional athlete, and I've dated a religious man, too, except he wasn't so *Godly.* Don't get me wrong, there are some religious and Godly men out there who are honest. *He just wasn't one of them.* I've dated a man who lied about his marital status. I've dated a guy I later learned was gay. I've dated men who were physically or verbally abusive towards me, and I once was engaged. I've been the ride or die chick. I've invested my time and money in a guy to later learn that he was using me for my *money* all along. I've been told by men that I'm beautiful, but the same men said they find my beauty to be intimidating to them. I haven't been on a date in over a year, and I haven't had sex in eleven months. I've found comfort in my vibrator whom I've named "Mood," because whenever I'm in the "Mood" my vibrator is my guy. A major plus is that I know "Mood" will never cheat on me, nor do I have to worry about contracting any STD's from "Mood." The sad truth is that the selection for men nowadays is slim, to none. At my age, they're either gay, married, don't believe in marriage at all, divorced and not looking to remarry, not married but already have children, or don't desire to have more children. They either carry a lot of baggage, play a lot of head games, have no ambition to be better in life, are too old or too young for me, or they're just too corny for my taste. I've even went as far as to date outside of my race, but still nothing (*Shaking my head*). The only relationship I haven't experienced is within my same sex. I'm not against anyone's love preference, but I have no intentions or any desire to be with another woman. After all the dating and failed relationships, I began questioning, *"Is something wrong with me, because I must be doing something wrong."* And for a long time, I began to believe that maybe being in a relationship or a marriage just wasn't for me after all. I sort of became content with being independent and alone. But I know that's not the way it's supposed to be. What really stresses me out the most, is that I know I am ambitious, smart, attractive and have a lot to offer. But I could never meet a guy that could offer me anything more than good sex or just a bunch of bullshit. I was in my last relationship on and off for three years. He was very indecisive about being with me or remaining in a relationship with his children's mother. I was blinded by my love for him. I waited three years for him to make a decision, and I continued to be in that on-and-off relationship with him. As a result, I became pregnant, and he asked me to abort our child. He expressed to me he didn't want any more children. But I made the conscious decision that I was keeping my baby, even if I had to do it all alone. Unfortunately, due to me constantly stressing out over him and his relationship with his children's mother, I miscarried, and I had to deal with those emotions on my own. He behaved as if the miscarriage never happened. *Whew!! The things that we go through as women to be loved by a man are unmatched.* He continued to be uncertain with his decision to be with me or his children's mother. He told me he didn't want to hurt his children by leaving her. But yet, he claimed I was the one he was in love with. So, I allowed him continued access to me, my body and my home. Although I knew he was sexually with his children's mother, too, *I settled.* There's always that one guy in every woman's life that she loves the most out of any man she's ever loved. He is usually the guy that caused her heart the most pain, hurt and damage. And no matter what he does to cause continued wounds to her heart, she finds it hard to emotionally move on from him, even when she's physically moved on in another relationship or is dating someone else because she hasn't had closure with him. And unfortunately, until she gets the closure she needs from him or finds closure within herself, no other man will ever have her heart that way again. He was that guy for me. We continued a sexual relationship up until eleven months ago. I finally got the confidence to leave him. He continued to call me, and there were times I was tempted by his words, and I missed him. I slipped and we had sex a few times. I knew nothing had changed with him. But I was horny, and I needed to feel more than just a vibrator. But after that last time, I knew I was finally done with him. Now that I'm about to turn forty, I feel that I haven't fulfilled half of my goals that I set when I first turned thirty. I assumed by this age I would have completed them. I feel that I've wasted so much time with the wrong people, and I feel so behind in my life. I'm going through changes in my body. My weight has fluctuated up and down this past year. I can't eat all the foods and desserts that I used to eat. I no longer can hang out all night the way I use to. I'm usually in the bed asleep by nine at night. During the day, when at work, all I think about is getting home to my pajamas and my comfortable bed. I don't desire to hang out like I use to. Even my circle of friends has changed. I don't know what my life is becoming. I think I'm going through a mid-life crisis. But whatever happens, I refuse to become that single woman who refers to her cat or dog as her children. I will not torment myself. I still want to have children of my own, and I still desire to be married one day. Damn! It's like I'm asking for too much. All I'm asking to find is real genuine love, and our love doesn't have to be perfect, just right for me. One second, I'm taking a deep breath. I need a full glass of wine after all of that. Because it's my birthday soon, everyone has been asking me if I'm planning to celebrate the big "Four Zero," and I've made it perfectly clear to everyone in my life that I don't want to make a huge deal about turning forty. But to my surprise, I found out that a surprise party is taking place for me this weekend. The only reason why I was told is because my friends who are throwing this surprise for me didn't want me to be caught off guard. I appreciate their gesture and for giving me a heads up. But I'm so frustrated that they put this surprise together for me. I'm not excited about turning forty. They don't understand what I'm mentally and emotionally going through right now. They haven't reached forty yet. I don't know. It just feels so different from when I was turning thirty. I enjoyed being in my thirties, because I felt that I had more time. I just knew by the time I reached forty I'd be married with children and happier. When it all boils down, I feel that I haven't accomplished a lot in my thirty-nine years. I made a plan to reach certain goals by forty, and I had a Bucket List of all the places I wanted to travel to by now. This Milestone is one mountain I don't look forward to climbing. I know my friends mean well, and I know they value our friendship. I'm just going through a lot emotionally right now. Will I be wrong if I choose not to attend my own party? I'm just not feeling up to being around anyone. I can use some honest advice right now.

Sincerely, Milestone

Dear Milestone,

The feelings that you're experiencing right now are normal. There isn't a woman on this earth that didn't dread turning a Milestone in her life. I remember when I was turning twenty-nine years old, I cried the entire day of my birthday because it was my last year of being in my twenties. I was not looking forward to my thirties. Like you, I felt old. I felt that I hadn't accomplished a lot of my goals, and I still desired to be married and have children one day. But I remember a wise woman showed me a different way to view it. She told me instead of looking at it as getting older, to look at it as becoming wiser. You are entering an age where you are becoming the best version of yourself. At forty, you begin to understand yourself and your body better. And you know without hesitation the things you want out of life, and you now call all of the shots whether people agree with it or not. You're entering an age where you will begin to value your time the most, and unlike in your past, you won't give it away as easily. All of a sudden, who you are becoming and all the things that you went through make sense to you. You begin to appreciate the life lessons and hurt that you went through because it helped sculpt you. The things that your parents tried to tell you about life just click. It's like having an epiphany. You wake up one day, and it just hits you. You no longer tolerate bullshit, excuse me, I mean *nonsense* from any man or anyone for that matter. Your confidence begins to grow and bloom in areas that you never thought you would find confidence within yourself. Unlike when you were in your thirties still trying to figure it out, when you enter your forties, you enter into a new chapter called "Now I know better." You begin to appreciate your curves and the parts of your body you once resented when you were in your thirties. You mature mentally, spiritually and emotionally. I know you're just getting ready to enter this stage in your life, but in due time, you will see and feel the difference within yourself and how you later view situations

187

and people. It's an experience and a feeling that's almost too hard for me to explain to you. But one thing I know for certain, turning forty doesn't put limitations on the goals or achievements you still desire to conquer. You can still have the husband, family and career you want and yes, even at age forty!! I promise that you will eventually find the man of your dreams. You are still young enough to have children, don't put a time clock on it. Never allow your age to limit what you're physically capable of still handling and doing. Your cocoon is opening, butterfly. One day, you'll be giving another young female similar advice. It's not the end for you; this is just the beginning. You needed to go through every heartbreak, hurt, disappointment and betrayal to become this woman you're becoming today. *Embrace her, she fought hard to get here.* Listen, you only turn forty once. It's a celebration that you should enjoy with the people who love you. This is more than just a Milestone. This is a new change in your life, and it only gets better from here. Go and enjoy your birthday celebration and eat all the cake you want. Then go and hit that gym. Happy Birthday and many more to come!

Sincerely, Gurlé

"Your past experiences helped you become the woman you are today. Embrace Her. She fought hard to become her!"

— Caprice Lamor —

Dear Proverbs 31 Woman,

I wanted to take this time to write you a letter. *Gurlé,* you have lived your life in excruciating pain, while uplifting others. You've cried secretly, yet smiled boldly in the faces of your peers, family and even strangers as if your heart was not bleeding from the stab wounds still lingering inside of you that were left behind by others. You've pretended to be who you weren't even when you didn't understand why you were pretending, when deep down inside you really wanted to scream and yell, *"SOMEBODY HELP ME!"* There is so much that I need to say to you. I understand now that a lot of things that happened to you as a child growing up were not your fault. But you carried a lot of hurt, baggage, pain, anger and resentment inside of you because of it. You've **blamed** yourself for every person in your life that made you cry. You've **blamed** yourself for choosing the wrong friendships, relationships and marriages. You've **blamed** yourself for them not telling you the truth, when all you really wanted was someone to just be REAL with you because you knew all the things that happened to you as a child and an adult weren't made up stories in your head. You just needed someone to confirm that what happened to you really did happen. You've **blamed** yourself for being rejected, misunderstood and unwanted. You've **blamed** your appearance, the way you looked for the reason why they wouldn't love you back. You've **blamed** yourself for being raped, sexually molested, and physically, emotionally, mentally and verbally abused. You've **blamed** yourself when your husband cheated on you and when your longtime boyfriend betrayed you and married another woman when you sacrificed years, patience, disappointments, hurt, financial struggles and gave your entire life to him. You've **blamed** yourself when a family member called you crazy and said that you were never going

191

to amount to anything in your life, and you carried it for years as fuel to motivate you, but yet it destroyed your confidence. You've **blamed** yourself for not having the body that men liked. And you damaged your body by over-dieting, going through unnecessary surgeries and by allowing social media to make you hate yourself for not looking perfect. You've **blamed** yourself for your parents giving you up for adoption, for neglecting you and for your parent's drug and alcohol abuse, or for not being present for you at all. You've **blamed** yourself for being too independent and for hiding your true sexual identity and love preferences. You've **blamed** yourself for not being able to conceive and have a child, for losing a child and/or for not wanting to have children at all. You've blamed yourself for not being popular enough and for not fitting in with the normal crowd. You've **blamed** yourself for being overlooked and rejected by your family and for being cast as the black sheep. You've **blamed** yourself for looking different because your parents' ethnicities were not the same. You've hated that you didn't look like everyone else. You've **blamed** yourself for feeling unloved; therefore, you wanted to kill yourself, and you fell into deep depression because of it. You've **blamed** yourself for the absence of your father and the broken relationship with your mother and/or the death of your parent/s. You've **blamed** yourself and tried to minimize who you were because people were jealous of you. You've **blamed** yourself for being a single mother raising a son or daughter alone, and you've been embarrassed and ashamed that you had to do it all alone. Your child/ren's father lied to you and promised to be there, but he left at the very beginning for another woman or another man. You've lost hope and trust, and you've lived most of your life surrounded by disappointment. BUT today, I owe **YOU** so many apologies.

Gurlé, I'm so sorry it took this long for you to realize your worth. I'm so sorry when he left you, you didn't understand you **DESERVED SO MUCH BETTER** and that God was preparing a **HUSBAND** for you. I'm sorry that when they rejected you, you didn't understand that God was really **PROTECTING** you from them. I'm sorry when they told you that you weren't pretty enough, you didn't understand you were created by God, and everything God created is **BEAUTIFUL.** I'm sorry for when you were raped, sexually, emotionally, verbally and physically abused, that you carried the pain all by yourself for so many years because you didn't know that when you gave it to God, he would **HEAL, RESTORE** and make you **WHOLE** again. I'm sorry for when they told you, you would never amount to anything in life, that you didn't know when God created you, he gave you **PURPOSE,** and that God said that you could do **ALL THINGS** through him who strengthens you. I'm sorry that when you chose the wrong friendships, relationships and marriages, you didn't know that God had to move the wrong people out of your life in order to bring the **RIGHT** people into your life. I am sorry that when you blamed yourself for looking different, that you didn't know that God made you **SPECIAL, ONE OF A KIND, UNIQUE and that God makes absolutely no mistakes.** I'm sorry that you didn't know when your parents gave you up for adoption, neglected and abandoned you, that God said when your parents reject you, he will **RECEIVE YOU.** I'm sorry you didn't know when you blamed yourself for not having the right body, that God made you **PERFECT** and **COMPLETE in him.** I'm sorry it took you this long to recognize who **YOU** are in God and who he created **YOU** to be in him. I'm sorry it took you this long to **FINALLY** love and accept **YOU,** your height, your hair color, your complexion, your personality, your genetics, your nationality, your ethnicity, your body and everything about this *Gurlé*! Yes, **YOU** are **ENOUGH! YOU** are **MORE** than sufficient. You have a **PURPOSE,** and you are **DESTINED**

193

to become the woman God created you to be. Despite all that you've been through in your life, **YOU STILL WON!** God is not finished with you yet. This is just the beginning. If no one else ever loves or accepts you, ever in your life, you have discovered **SELF LOVE** within **YOURSELF**, the **LOVE** of **GOD** inside of **YOU**. Last, but not least, I owe you a HUGE apology. **I AM SORRY, AND I FORGIVE MYSELF.**

Sincerely, Proverbs 31 Woman

You're now ready to fly…Butterfly

Dear Gurlé
You Are
Beautiful!

Much Love Always
Caprice Lamn

49910746R00126